FRANKIE FOSTER

Pick 'n' Mix

Here to Help!

Also by Jean Ure

Frankie Foster: Fizzy Pop!

Ice Lolly

Love and Kisses

Fortune Cookie

Star Crazy Me!

Over the Moon

Boys Beware

Sugar and Spice

Is Anybody There?

Secret Meeting

Passion Flower

Shrinking Violet

Boys on the Brain

Pumpkin Pie

Skinny Melon and Me

Becky Bananas, This is Your Life!

Fruit and Nutcase

The Secret Life of Sally Tomato

Family Fan Club

Special three-in-one editions

The Tutti-Frutti Collection

The Flower Power Collection

The Friends Forever Collection

FRANKIE FOSTER

Pick 'n' Mix

Here to Help!

Jean Ure

HarperCollins Children's Books

First published in Great Britain by HarperCollins *Children's Books* 2011
HarperCollins *Children's Books* is a division of HarperCollins*Publishers* Ltd,
77–85 Fulham Palace Road, Hammersmith, London W6 8JB

The HarperCollins *Children's Books* website address is
www.harpercollins.co.uk

Jean Ure's website is
www.jeanure.com

1

FRANKIE FOSTER: Pick 'n' Mix
Text copyright © Jean Ure 2011

The author asserts the moral right to be identified as the author of this work.

ISBN-13 978-0-00-736267-7

Typeset by Palimpsest Book Production Ltd, Falkirk, Stirlingshire
Printed and bound in England by Clays Ltd, St Ives plc

MIX
Paper from
responsible sources
FSC
www.fsc.org **FSC® C007454**

FSC is a non-profit international organisation established to promote the
responsible management of the world's forests. Products carrying the FSC
label are independently certified to assure consumers that they come
from forests that are managed to meet the social, economic and
ecological needs of present and future generations.

Find out more about HarperCollins and the environment at
www.harpercollins.co.uk/green

For Rebecca Cross and Amy Saunders,

who have been so helpful

I didn't mean to cut a hole in my bedroom carpet...

CHAPTER
ONE

I didn't mean to cut a hole in my bedroom carpet. Not that I'm claiming it was an accident, exactly, though it could have been. Like if I'd tripped over the edge of the bed, for instance, with Dad's Stanley knife clutched in my hand, the blade might well have gone plunging into the carpet all by itself and carved a huge great chunk out of it. I mean, that is what could quite easily have happened.

I'm not saying that it *did*; just that it could have.

All I'm saying is, I didn't set out to cut a hole. It wasn't like I woke up in the morning and thought, "Today I shall cut a hole in my carpet." It just seemed like a good idea at the time, as things so often do. Then afterwards you wonder why, only by then it's too late. This is something that happens to me rather a lot. I am quite unfortunate in that way.

What I was doing, in actual fact, wasn't thinking about cutting holes so much as trying to find a way of fitting my corner cabinet into a corner. Gran had given me the cabinet when she moved out of her house into a flat. It's really cute! Very small and painted white, with pink and blue flowers all running round the edge, and tiny glass-panelled doors. Gran used to keep china ornaments in there. Shepherdesses and milkmaids and old-fashioned ladies selling balloons. I keep my collection of shells and fossils and interesting stones with holes in them. Gran knew I'd always loved her corner cabinet. I was so excited when she gave it to me! But the thing is, it is a *corner* cabinet. That is why it is shaped like a triangle. It has to stand in a *corner.*

I've only got two corners in my bedroom. This is because it's the smallest room in the house, tucked away under the roof, and is shaped like a wedge of cheese. The big front bedroom is Mum and Dad's; the one at the back is Angel's; the little one over the garage is Tom's; and the one the size of a broom cupboard belongs to me. Mum says that when Angel goes to Uni, Tom can have her room and I can have his. And when *Tom* goes to Uni, I can take my pick. But since Angel is only fifteen, it seems to me I'm going to be stuck in my broom cupboard for years to come.

I don't really mind; I quite like my little bedroom. It's cosy, like a nest. And I love the way the roof slopes down, and the way the window is at floor level. The only problem is, the lack of corners! My bed is in one, and my wardrobe in the other. I'd tried fitting Gran's cabinet into the angle between the roof and the floor, but it was just the tiniest little bit too tall. If I could only slice a couple of centimetres off the bottom of it...

That was when it came to me. If I couldn't slice anything off Gran's cabinet, how about cutting a hole in the carpet? It just seemed like the obvious solution. What Dad calls *lateral thinking*. I reckoned he would be quite pleased with me. He is always telling us to "think outside the box" and "use your imagination". That was exactly what I was doing!

I left Rags on the bed – Rags is our dog, though mostly he belongs to me – and went rushing downstairs to fetch Dad's carpet-cutting knife from the kitchen drawer. It was Sunday morning, which meant everyone was at home, but fortunately neither Mum nor Dad seemed to be about. I say fortunately as they both (though 'specially Mum) have this inconvenient habit of demanding to know why you want things. Angel is bad enough. She was in the kitchen eating yoghurt and painting her toenails. She looked at me like I was some kind of criminal.

"What are you doing with that knife?" she said.

I said, "What knife?"

"That knife you've put up your sleeve."

"Oh!" I said. "That." And I gave this little laugh, to show that I was amused.

"That's Dad's Stanley knife, that is. You're not supposed to play with it."

"For your information," I said, loftily, "I am not *playing* with it."

"So what d'you want it for?"

"Ha!" I said. "Wouldn't you like to know?"

Angel looked at me with narrowed eyes. "You'd better not be getting up to anything," she said.

I gave this manic laugh. She gets me like that at times. Always so *bossy*. So *interfering*. What was it to her, what I got up to?

As I left the kitchen, I bumped into Tom on his way in.

"She's got Dad's Stanley knife," said Angel.

Tom grunted. It is his way of carrying on a "Uh?" conversation.

He has upward grunts, like "Uh." and downward grunts, like "*Uh.*"

"I want to cut something," I said.

Tom said, "Uh."

I do occasionally wonder whether Tom might be some kind of alien from outer space, but at least he is not bossy and he never, *ever* interferes. Mum says he is the strong and silent type. I wish my sister was the silent type! She is one of those people, she just can't stop her tongue from clacking.

"On your own head be it!" she yelled, as I went back up the hall.

Dunno what she meant by that. Mostly, I take no notice of her.

I made a really good job of cutting a hole. I cut it triangular, to fit the cabinet. What I did, I stood the cabinet on a sheet of newspaper, then I marked all the way round with a felt tip pen, so I had a pattern, then I cut out the pattern and put it on the carpet and cut round the edge of it with Dad's knife. I know it is wrong to boast, but I couldn't help feeling a sense of pride. Mum always accuses me of being slapdash.

"You don't take enough care, Frankie!"

But I took care of my hole! It worked like a dream; Gran's cabinet was a perfect fit. Nobody would ever know I'd had to take a bit out of the carpet. There was only one slight problem, and that wasn't my fault: the carpet seemed to be fraying, and coming apart where I'd cut it. Long fronds of nylon had started waving about.

Rags, who'd been lying on my bed watching me work, came bounding over to have a look. I told him to go away. I didn't want his big furry head pushing itself in while I chopped off the fronds.

"Here," I said. "Have this!"

I gave him the triangle of carpet to chew, and he jumped back happily on the bed with it.

"Good boy," I said.

He *is* a good boy. Angel complains that he is too big and clumping, and that he smells when he gets wet, but she is only miffed cos she wanted a rabbit.

I'd just started to snip off some of the fronds

when there was a knock at the door and Tom's head appeared.

"Gotta come downstairs," he said.

I was immediately suspicious. I said, "Why?"

"Mum wants you."

"What for?" What had I done *now*? Honestly, I get the blame for everything in our house. Only the other day Mum accused me of breaking her flour sifter, just because I'd borrowed it to sift some earth for my wormery that I was making. All I can say is, it wasn't broken when I put it back in the cupboard. I'm sure it wasn't. But just, like, automatically, it has to be my fault.

"Is she cross?" I said.

Tom said, "Uh?"

"Cos I haven't done anything!"

"Uh."

Unless Angel had gone and told her about the knife?

Mum, Frankie's gone off with Dad's knife! She says she's going to cut something.

Mum gets really fussed about stuff like that. Stuff you read about in the papers. People being stabbed and everything. But I wouldn't ever, *ever,* take a knife out of the house. I know better than that! I'm not stupid. I just needed it to cut a hole in my carpet. "You coming, or what?" said Tom.

I clumped reluctantly behind him down the stairs. It was slowly occurring to me that maybe Mum wasn't going to be too happy when she discovered what I'd done. If Angel hadn't gone and told her about the knife, she wouldn't ever have had to know. It wasn't like it was obvious. Nobody was going to go into my bedroom and cry, "Ooh, look, there's a hole in the carpet!" But if Angel had gone and opened her big clattering mouth...

Mum was in the kitchen, sitting at the table.

Dad was also there. *Angel* was there. This looked serious.

"I haven't done anything," I said.

Angel gave a short screech of laughter. She sounds quite mad when she does that. I think, actually, she is a bit mad. (I mean mad loopy, not mad angry, though she's usually that as well.)

"Take a seat," said Mum. "And don't look so worried! This isn't about anything you may or may not have done. It's a family conference. Tom, come and sit down! Don't drape yourself over the sink. Right. OK! Now, then... you know my lady Mrs Duffy?"

I knew Mrs Duffy; she was one of Mum's customers. Mum always refers to them as her ladies. They come to have hems taken up, and dresses made, and zips put in. Tom was looking blank. He never really notices people; only stuff that's on his computer screen.

"Mrs Duffy's the big lady," I said.

Angel sucked in her breath. "That is *so* not the sort of thing to say!"

I didn't see why. Mrs Duffy *is* big. Like Angel is thin as a pin. But it didn't seem quite the right moment for starting an argument, so I ignored her and informed Tom that, "She has a daughter called Emilia."

Tom said, "Uh?"

"Mum made her a special dewdrop outfit for her school's dressing up day. She looked really sweet! Didn't she, Mum?"

"She did," said Mum. "And in fact it's Emilia we have to talk about."

I sat up straight and arranged my face into its listening shape. It's the face I use in class when I want a teacher to know that I am paying attention and taking everything in. I liked the idea of talking about Emilia. Far better than talking about me and something I might or might not have done.

Mum explained how Mrs Duffy was going to have to go into hospital for an operation.

"She'll be in for about two weeks, then she'll need at least another two to get her strength back. She's really worried about what's going to happen to Emilia. She'd normally go to her nan's, but her nan's had a stroke and has had to go into a home, and her dad's no longer on the scene, so that means she's going to have to be fostered, which for a girl like poor little Emilia is really problematic."

Tom said, "Uh?"

"She has learning difficulties," said Mum. "And she's never been away from home before, except to stay with her nan. Her mum's in quite a state about it. So, I was wondering... how would you feel about Emilia coming to us? At least that way she'd be with people she knows. Well, she knows me, and she knows Frankie. It would really set Mrs Duffy's mind at rest. On the other hand..." Mum paused. "I have to say that your dad is a bit dubious about it, but I need to know how you three feel. Angel?"

Angel shrugged. "I guess it'd be OK. So long as I'm not expected to *do* anything. I mean, how old is she?"

"She's thirteen," said Mum. "But she's very young for her age. More like an eight-year-old. Tom? How about you?"

Tom said, "Uh?" And then, "Yeah. Fine."

"Frankie?"

"I think she should *definitely* come," I said.

"There is just one thing," said Mum. "How would you and Angel feel about sharing a bedroom?"

I don't know who was more appalled, me or Angel.

"You've got to be joking!" shrieked Angel.

"They'd end up throttling each other," said Dad.

"I'd throttle *her*," said Angel, casting me a venomous look. "Mum, please! I can't have her coming and messing up my bedroom!"

Mum sighed. "I thought you'd say that."

"Well, honestly! You know what she's like."

I might have retorted that I knew what she was like, screaming blue murder if anyone just dared to even *breathe* on any of her precious bits and pieces, but an idea had come whizzing into my brain.

"If Angel moved into my room," I said, "me and Emilia could share hers!"

"You'd still mess things up," snapped Angel.

"No, I wouldn't, cos you could take everything out so's I couldn't contaminate it."

Angel said, "Huh!" Mum looked at me, doubtfully.

"Frankie, are you sure?"

"I don't mind sharing," I said. "Just so long as it's not with *her.*"

Angel stuck up a finger. This is *such* a rude thing to do. And Mum let her get away with it! I bet she wouldn't have let me.

"Angel, could you bear to move into Frankie's room?" she said. "Just for a few weeks? I know it's asking a lot of you, but..."

We all waited. I could see the struggle going on inside Angel's head. She hated the thought of me being in possession of her room while she was banished to my humble broom cupboard, but she obviously didn't want to be thought mean or uncharitable. In the end, rather grumpily, she said, "I s'ppose I wouldn't mind."

"That's really good of you," said Mum. "I really appreciate that! Mrs Duffy will be so relieved."

"Can I go now?" said Angel.

"Yes, yes! Off you go."

Angel and Tom disappeared upstairs, Dad went off to his shed.

"So when will Emilia be coming?" I said.

"Some time in the week; Tuesday or Wednesday, I think. I won't move you into Angel's room until the last minute. But Frankie, I have to ask, are you really quite certain about this? Emilia's a sweet girl, but it's not going to be easy. She's not like an ordinary thirteen-year-old."

"No problem," I said. "I'll look after her. It'll be good training!" I plan to be a social worker when I leave school. Either that or an aromatherapist. At any rate, something to do with helping people. Mum knows this. "I reckon the sooner I get started," I said, "the better."

"Well… so long as you're sure."

I told Mum that I was absolutely positive and went galloping back upstairs to admire my corner cabinet standing in its corner. It was a pity I wasn't going to get the benefit of it for the next few weeks, but Angel needn't think she was putting *her* stuff in there. I wasn't turning out my fossil collection just for her.

I got a bit of a shock when I went into my room: a long bald strip of carpet had appeared between the cabinet and the bed. It was Rags! He'd discovered the loose fronds and was joyously tugging at them, making happy little growly noises, his bum stuck up in the air.

"What are you *doing*?" I shrieked. Rags started, guiltily. "Bad!" I said. "Bad!"

Rags rolled an eye, and grinned, then collapsed on to his back and frantically waved his paws at me. Poor little man! How could I be cross with him? It wasn't his fault. All the same, it was a nasty moment. Mum could hardly be expected to miss a long bald strip in the middle of my carpet. I didn't even have a rug I could use for covering it up. In the end, in desperation, I grabbed a pile of clothes and chucked them on the floor. I knew Mum wouldn't clear them away cos she'd told me only last week she wasn't going to tidy up after me any more.

"You must learn to be a bit more responsible. I'm not here to act as your servant."

I was safe for the moment, but I knew it couldn't last. Sooner or later I was going to be moved into Angel's room and Angel was going to be moved into mine, and then the baldness would be revealed in all its horror. *And* the hole in the carpet. It was fraying fast, all round the edge, and was ballooning out where Rags had tugged.

There was only one thing to do. I raced back downstairs and into the kitchen.

"Mum?"

Where was she? I had to get to her before she rang Mrs Duffy.

"Mum!" I ran, panting, up the hall.

"What is it?" said Mum, coming out of the front room. "Is the house on fire?"

I said, "No, but I've been thinking... maybe it's not fair on Angel, me moving into her room. You know how she hates people touching her things."

"Well, that's all right," said Mum. "Don't touch them."

"But she hates me even just looking at them. Just *breathing* on them. It might give her a nervous breakdown!"

"She'll get over it," said Mum.

"But it could be fatal!"

"I doubt it."

I was really surprised at Mum. Who would have thought she could be so heartless?

I said, "*Mu-u-um!*"

"It's no big deal," said Mum. "So she's sacrificing her bedroom for four weeks. It won't do her any harm. I'm more concerned about you; Emilia can be quite clingy. I just hope you're not biting off more than you can chew."

"*I'm* not," I said. "It's Angel I'm worried about."

"That's very sweet of you," said Mum, "but really quite unnecessary. In any case, it's too late now, I've already rung Mrs Duffy. Emilia's coming on Tuesday."

I said, "Oh."

"We'll do the move tomorrow evening."

"OK." I trailed to the door, then suddenly turned back. "Maybe Emilia could sleep in my room, with me?"

"Don't be silly," said Mum. "We couldn't get a second bed in your room."

"I could always sleep downstairs," I said. Emilia by herself probably wouldn't even notice a hole in the carpet. "I could sleep on the sofa!"

"Now you're just being ridiculous," said Mum.

"But, M—"

"You're both sleeping in Angel's room! That's it, it's all sorted."

"B—"

"*Frankie!*"

I was doomed.

CHAPTER TWO

"So then Mum said how would we feel if she came to live with us for a bit, and I said I wouldn't mind, except if it meant sharing a bedroom with Angel, cos you know what *she's* like."

Jemma said, *"Yuck, yes!"*

Skye nodded, wisely. "Wouldn't work."

"Well, this is it," I said. "I mean, *imagine.*"

It was Monday afternoon and we were

walking back from school. Skye and Jem are my best mates. I'd been bursting all day to tell them about what had happened to my carpet and the terrible trouble I was going to be in, but what with one thing and another this was the first chance I'd had.

"Anyway," I said, "I got this bright idea? I said if Angel moved into my room, me and her could share Angel's room—"

"You and this girl?"

"Emilia. Yes! But—"

"What's she like?"

"Oh –" I waved a hand. "She's all right." Emilia wasn't what I wanted to talk about. What I wanted to talk about was this fearsome thing that was hanging over me. The hole in my carpet... "I don't actually know her very well. The thing is—"

"Suppose you don't get on?" said Jem.

"We'll get on! It's only for a few weeks." I'm

not like Angel, I don't get all fussed and bothered about stuff. Angel is always on about her 'stuff' and how no one's got to touch it. "The thing *is*—"

"Could seem like for ever," said Skye.

"Well, it won't, cos it's not! The awful thing *is* she's coming tomorrow and tonight we're going to swap bedrooms and Mum's going to discover there's a hole in my carpet!"

The words wailed out of me. There was a silence. Then Skye, very solemnly, said, "A hole."

"In my carpet!"

They looked at each other.

"You mean it's, like, threadbare?" said Jem.

"No! I cut it."

"You what?" said Skye.

"I cut it!"

"Cut your carpet?"

Honestly! It is so annoying when people keep repeating everything you say.

"Yes," I snapped. "I cut my carpet!"

"But why?"

"Cos I wanted Gran's cabinet to fit in the corner and the ceiling wasn't high enough!"

"So you cut the carpet."

Really, for someone who is supposed to have this immense great brain, always getting A pluses and coming top of everything, Skye can be incredibly slow on the uptake. How many more times did I have to tell her? *Yes, I cut the carpet!*

"It would have been all right," I said, "if it hadn't gone and frayed round the edges. Nobody would have noticed. It was Rags that messed things up. He tugged at it. He's made a bald patch!"

"Dunno what to say," said Skye.

Jem sniggered. "Bet her mum'll find something!"

She thought that was *funny*? One of my best friends thought it was *funny* that Mum was going to be mad at me? I glared at her.

"Well, sorry," said Jem, "but really! You do the stupidest things."

I resented that. "It wasn't stupid," I said, "it was the logical solution. If you can't make the ceiling *higher*, you make the floor *lower*. I was just being practical! You can't have a corner cabinet not standing in a corner."

"Of course you can't," said Skye, soothingly. "You did what anyone would have done... *you cut a hole in your carpet!*"

She and Jem both fell about.

"It was only small," I pleaded.

"Only small!" shrieked Jem, clutching herself round the middle.

"Now it's this size –" Skye held her arms out in a circle. They collapsed on each other, helpless with foolish giggles.

Crossly, I said, "How was I to know it would start unravelling?"

"Unravelling!" squeaked Jem.

Screech. Hoot. These were supposed to be my *friends*.

Skye wiped her eyes on the back of her hand. "Maybe you could say it was Rags that made the hole."

"And get a poor little innocent dog into trouble? I couldn't do that! In any case," I said, "you can tell it's been cut." Not meaning to boast, I added that I had made a proper pattern. "I cut right round the edge of it with Dad's knife. The one he uses for carpets. It's really sharp! I was ever so careful, cos I didn't want to cut myself. I just wanted my cabinet to go in a corner!"

"And now it's in one," said Skye, soothingly.

"Yes, but there's a great bald patch!" I explained how for the moment I'd hidden the bald patch beneath a pile of clothes. "But Angel's like this real tidiness freak? She'll want it all cleared up. I tried suggesting me and Emilia share my room, I even offered to sleep downstairs, like on the sofa or something, so's Emilia could have the room to herself, cos she probably wouldn't mind a few clothes lying about the floor, but M—"

"How old is this girl?" said Jem.

I looked at her, annoyed. I felt like saying, "Pardon me, but I was in the middle of speaking." It is really bad manners to interrupt a person.

"Emilia," said Jem. "How old is she?"

"She's thirteen, but—"

"*Thirteen?* You mean she's Year 9?" Skye pulled a face. We were only Year 7 and most Year 9s, at our school at any rate, treated us like snot.

"I dunno what year she's in. She has learning difficulties so she's more like an eight year old? She goes to St Giles." St Giles is the special school just a bit further down the road from where we go. "I expect probably she'll need a bit of looking after."

Skye said, "What kind of looking after?"

"Well – you know! Just making sure she's OK. I promised Mum we'd be responsible for her."

"*Us?*" Skye was starting to sound a bit alarmed.

"She's ever so sweet," I said. "She won't be any trouble."

"You reckon?"

"It'll just be, like, seeing her to school and picking her up again, checking she doesn't get lost. That kind of thing. Actually," I said, "I'm quite looking forward to it." Well, I *had* been.

 Just at the moment all I could think of was what Mum was going to say.

Jem put her arm through mine. "I don't mind helping look after her," she said.

I beamed at her, gratefully; at least I had the support of one of my friends. Skye was gnawing at her lip, her forehead all crinkled. She is such a pessimist! If I listened to what she had to say I would never go anywhere or do anything. I suppose it is what comes of having this massive great brain, like a computer. Instead of just looking straight ahead, she whizzes frantically about, all up and down the side roads, in and out of blind alleys, searching for things that could go wrong. A bit too complicated for my liking. I think I am quite a straightforward type, though Mum would probably say I tend to act without thinking, which is what she said when I accidentally set fire to Dad's garden shed and *almost certainly* what she was going to say when I tried to explain why I'd cut a hole in my carpet...

I gulped as we reached Sunnybrook Gardens, which is where the three of us go our different ways.

"Wish me luck," I said.

"What for?" said Jem. "Oh! Yes. Your carpet."

She giggled. "Hope your mum doesn't get too mad!"

"Blame it on Rags," urged Skye.

Maybe I could. After all, it was *sort* of his fault. If he hadn't chewed the fronds I could have snipped them off and nobody would ever have known. I could tell Mum that I'd cut the hole *after* he'd done his chewing. I could say I'd been trying to tidy things up and the knife had slipped, so then I'd thought I might as well make the hole triangle-shaped and put the cabinet on top of it. Yes! That would work.

I crashed through the front door, all prepared with my story (in case Mum had already made the dreaded discovery and was waiting for me like a great hovering cloud at the top of the stairs). But then Rags came bounding down the hall, full of his usual doggy ecstasy at seeing me again, and I knew that I just couldn't do it.

"It's all right," I whispered. "I won't blame you!"

While me and Rags were having a hug-in, the door of the front room opened and Mum looked out.

"Oh, Frankie, there you are. I'll be with you in a minute, I'm just seeing one of my ladies. You and Angel go and make a start on your bedrooms. Tell Angel she doesn't have to move every last item... concentrate on clothes."

I said, "OK." Trying to make like it was no big deal and that my heart wasn't already starting to sink like a lead balloon.

Angel was in the kitchen, texting someone. She is always texting. I said, "Mum wants us to get on with moving things."

Angel pulled a face.

"She says not every last item. Just clothes, mainly."

Angel said, "If you think I'm leaving all my stuff for you to get your grubby hands on—"

There was a pause, while she went on texting.

I said, "What if I do?"

Irritably, she said, "Do what?"

"Think what you just said."

"Then you'd better think again!" Angel snapped her phone shut and went flouncing ahead of me, up the hall. "Let's get this over with. And you can clear up all your mess," she added.

I said, "What mess?"

"The mess in your room."

"How do you know there's any mess in my room?"

"Cos there always is. Just because I have to exist in a cupboard for the next few weeks doesn't mean I have to live in a *tip*."

I sniffed as I went up the extra little flight of stairs to my room. The clothes were still on the floor, where I'd left them. I was about to pick them up when I had another of my bright ideas. It just struck me suddenly, as these things do. I think I must have a very active sort of brain.

I left the clothes where they were, seized an armful of stuff from the wardrobe and went plunging down to Angel's room, crossing paths with Angel on the way back up.

"*Mess*," she said, as she came back down. "What are you doing with that rug?"

"I thought you ought to take it with you. Cos, you know, I might spill stuff on it or something."

"Good thinking," said Angel.

I galloped back up, kicked the clothes out of the way, and carefully laid the rug on top of the bald patch. It looked a bit odd, cos of sticking out at an angle, but at least it covered things up. It would have been perfectly all right if Angel hadn't gone and interfered. She came in with another load of clothes, took one look at the rug and said, "It's supposed to go *here*, by the side of the bed."

"That's boring," I said. "That's where everybody has them."

"Yes, for a reason," said Angel. "It's where they *go*."

"Not if you're being creative."

She isn't creative; that is the problem. I don't think she has very much in the way of imagination. Before I could stop her she'd snatched up the rug, revealing the bald patch in all its horror. I cringed. I'd been secretly hoping that by some miracle it might have shrunk a bit during the day, but if anything it seemed to have grown even worse.

Angel shrieked, *"Oh my God!"*

That was the moment when Mum appeared in the doorway.

"Now what?" she said. There was a distinct note of tetchiness in her voice – and that was *before* she'd seen the bald patch. It didn't bode well. "Don't tell me you two are at it already?"

Angel said nothing; just pointed, with quivering finger. Mum walked to the end of the bed. She looked. There was a rather nasty moment of silence.

"All right," said Mum. She took a long, deep breath, like she was counting to ten. "So how did it happen?"

"It wasn't Rags' fault!" I said. "He found some loose ends and he tugged on them!"

Mum's eyes followed the trail from the edge of the bed to the base of the cabinet.

"These loose ends?" More fronds had sprouted overnight; a whole forest of them, short and bristly. "Frankie," said Mum, "*what* have you been doing?"

I tried my best to explain. All about the

45

cabinet and the lack of corners. How I hadn't actually set *out* to cut a hole.

"You mean, it just happened? All by itself?" Mum shook her head. She didn't sound cross; just kind of... defeated. "Words fail me," she said.

It's a pity they can't fail Angel occasionally. I have never known anyone go on like she does.

"Well, that's it," she said. "I'm not living in this tip! You can just get your stinky clothes out of my room and bring them back up here. Look at it! Look at the state of it! How could I invite any of my friends round? They'd think we were too poor to have decent carpets!"

"We are," said Mum. "That's what I find so depressing. I don't know what your dad's going to say, my girl, but you'd better brace yourself. He's not going to be best pleased."

"She's a vandal!" shrilled Angel. She swept a

load of clothes out of the wardrobe and marched across to the door.

"Where do you think you're going?" said Mum.

"Going back to my own room!"

"You'll do no such thing. You come back here! You agreed to swap."

"That was before she hacked the carpet to bits. Why should I be expected to live in squalor?"

"Oh, for goodness' sake, stop being so melodramatic," said Mum. "You're only going to be in here for a few weeks, it won't kill you."

I knew what Angel's game was. She hadn't really wanted to swap rooms in the first place; she was just using the carpet as an excuse. Mum obviously knew it too, cos she told her sharply to pull herself together.

"Put those clothes back and go and get the rest of them. And you, Frankie, start clearing your drawers. Let's at least get the job done before your dad arrives home. You'd better be prepared. It may well be," said Mum, "that he'll decide to stop your pocket money for the next few months until we've saved enough to replace the carpet."

"Dunno why you'd bother," said Angel. "Might just as well put down a load of straw."

"I wouldn't mind straw," I said.

"No, you'd probably be happier in it... then you could wallow, like a *pig.*"

Angel went banging off down the stairs. I shouted after her: "I like pigs!"

"I wouldn't get too cocky if I were you," said Mum. "That's Dad's van I just heard pulling in. Do you want me to break the news, or would you prefer to tell him yourself?"

"Rather you did it," I mumbled.

"That's probably a wise choice," said Mum.

CHAPTER
THREE

Sometimes my dad can be so lovely! He wasn't anywhere near as cross as I'd thought he'd be. I reckon Mum was a bit put out. She's always complaining that she's the one that has to keep telling us off, and that just now and again it ought to be Dad's turn. This was definitely his turn. But when I rather desperately explained about the lack of corners, and my bedroom ceiling not being high enough, he laughed. He actually laughed. Mum gave him such a look.

"*Well,*" said Dad, "now I've heard everything!"

"Hacking her carpet to bits," grumbled Mum.

"Not good," agreed Dad. "Definitely not good. But I have to admit, there's a certain muddle-headed logic to it."

I don't know why he said that. *Muddle-headed.* What was muddled about it?

I told him that I'd been using my imagination. "Like you always say we should. *Don't just give up, look for a solution.* That's what you're always telling us."

"True," said Dad.

Mum made an impatient huffing noise. "So what do we do about the carpet?"

"She'll have to live with it."

"Like that will be any hardship." Mum said it rather bitterly. "She already exists in a tip, as it is."

"Well, that's her problem. I guess we should just think ourselves lucky she didn't go for the other option."

"What's the other option?" I said.

"Cutting a hole in the ceiling?"

"Oh!" I was entranced. "I never thought of that."

"Precisely! Let us be thankful for small mercies."

"I can't say I'm exactly brimming over with gratitude," snapped Mum. "One perfectly good carpet ruined, and Angel in a sulk, which is all we need."

Dad said, "What's she in a sulk about?"

"Having to live in a pig sty for the next four weeks. And who could blame her?"

Mum left the room, obviously in somewhat of a huff.

"There, now," said Dad. "You've really upset her. You'd better go and apologise."

I said, "I have apologised!"

"Well, do it again. And make sure you mean it! The only reason I'm being as lenient as I am – which is far more than you deserve – is that I'm proud of you for offering to help out with Emilia."

I glowed. I love it when Dad is proud of me! It doesn't happen that often.

"It'll be like work experience," I said.

"I suppose that's one way of looking at it. I just hope you're not taking on more than you can handle."

I said, "Da-a-ad!" Why did everyone doubt me? First Mum, then Skye, now Dad. "I know what I'm doing!"

"Yes, and I'm sure you mean well," said Dad. "But from what I can gather, Emilia is quite a handful."

"Dad, she's sweet! And we couldn't let her go to strangers."

Dad ruffled my hair. "This is why I'm letting you off lightly. But please don't go cutting any more carpets!"

Jem and Skye were waiting for me as usual next morning, on the corner of Sunnybrook Gardens.

"So what happened?" cried Jem. "Was your mum furious?"

"You'd better believe it," I said.

"Not surprised." Jem giggled. "Cutting holes in your carpet!"

"Is she going to make you pay for it?" said Skye.

"No." I twirled, triumphantly. "She wanted to. She tried to get Dad to say he was going to stop my pocket money, but Dad just laughed. He thought it was funny."

"*Funny?*"

"He said it showed logical thinking." I didn't add the bit about muddle-headed; it didn't seem quite necessary. "He told Mum they just had to be grateful I hadn't made a hole in the ceiling."

Jem crinkled her nose. "Why would you have done that?"

"Cos of it being the other option?"

Jem looked at me, doubtfully. She doesn't have a logical brain like me.

"If you can't make the floor *lower*," I said, "you make the ceiling *higher*. Right?"

"How d'you make a ceiling higher?"

"Dunno. With a drill, I s'ppose."

"I bet even your dad would get mad then!"

"Maybe."

"I reckon he spoils you." Skye said it rather sternly. "My dad wouldn't let me get away with cutting holes in things."

Skye wouldn't cut holes in things. She might have an enormous brain, but she is not in the least bit practical. I told her that Dad liked to encourage us to use our imagination, and to find ways round our problems.

"Anyhow," I said, "he's pleased cos of me saying I'll look after Emilia. She's coming this afternoon, Mum's going to pick her up."

"Ooh, can we come and see her?" said Jem.

I hesitated.

"*Please*, Frankee! Can we?"

"It might p'raps be better if you waited till tomorrow." I didn't want to put her off, but I had this feeling Mum might accuse us of crowding if all three of us turned up. "She'll probably be a bit, like, confused just at first?"

"Exactly," said Skye. She gave Jem a shove. "Stop being so pushy."

"*Me* being pushy? Huh! I like that," said Jem.

They bickered happily all the way to school. Normally I'd have joined in, but I was thinking about Emilia, wondering just how much looking after she was going to need. I didn't really, properly know her; only just to say hello to when she'd come round with her mum. I couldn't even have said how old she was, until Mum told me. I'd never have guessed she was thirteen. She was the right size for thirteen, but she didn't look thirteen. She didn't behave like thirteen. More like eight was what Mum had said. Thinking back to when I was eight, which was only quite a short time ago, I couldn't remember that I'd needed any looking after. I'd gone to and from school by myself, I'd gone to the shops by myself, I'd even taken Rags up the park by myself. But both Mum and Dad seemed to think Emilia would need special treatment and that I would have to keep an eye on her.

Well, that was all right! I could do that. 'Specially with Jem being so eager to help. Skye obviously wasn't that keen. Unlike me and Jem, she is not really a people person. She can sometimes be a bit prickly and awkward. But I wasn't too worried. After all, we were friends and friends do things together.

I galloped home at the end of school to find that Mum and Emilia had just arrived. Mum said, "Emilia, this is Frankie. You know Frankie, don't you?" Emilia gave a big banana beam and held out her hand.

"I'm Melia," she said.

I shook her hand and said, "Hi, Melia."

Mum shot me a suspicious glance in case I was making fun, but I wasn't! It just came out like that: Melia. It seemed more friendly than *Emilia*.

"Come and meet the others." Mum led the way round the back. "They're probably in the kitchen. Oh, and Frankie, can you grab hold of Rags and not let him jump up? In fact, it might be a good idea if you shut him out for a bit. It won't hurt him to stay in the garden."

"Mum," I said, "that's not fair!" It was his home as much as anybody's. Why should he be sent into exile? "He'll be all right, I'll keep hold of him."

"Well, just make sure that you do."

"He won't hurt you," I told Melia. I hoped she wasn't going to be silly about dogs. "He's very good-natured."

Melia gave another beam. Her mouth split into two and went curving right up towards her ears. It was kind of infectious. It made me want to beam as well.

"Honestly, he's just playful," I said.

While me and Rags were having our usual hug-in, Melia introduced herself to Tom and Angel. She had this really penetrating voice, like it was coming through a loud hailer. She didn't so much talk as SHOUT. She held out her hand, like she had with me.

"I'm Melia!"

She certainly wasn't shy. I began to think that maybe Jem and Skye could have come round after all.

I could see that Tom and Angel didn't know what to make of her. Angel looked confused, like she'd never seen a hand held out before and wasn't sure what she was supposed to do with it. Tom just grunted. He did it twice: once up, and once down.

"Uh? Uh."

Melia giggled. She had a strange, gurgling sort of giggle, like water glugging down a plughole. Tom turned pink. Angel shot a reproachful glance at Mum, like, *How could you do this to us?* Personally I thought it was quite funny.

I didn't think it was quite so funny when Rags, attracted by the gurgling, suddenly broke off from cuddling with me, went bounding across to Melia and almost sent her flying. He doesn't mean to be rough, but he is a big dog and sometimes his enthusiasm runs away with him. I rushed to grab him before Mum could yell at me to "Put that dog outside!" or before Melia could start screaming. If she started screaming Mum would be really mad at me. She was still in something of a sulk about the carpet.

"Frankie," she said, "I warned you! Put that—"

She never got around to saying the rest of it cos to everyone's surprise, including mine, Melia had wrapped both arms round Rags' neck and was energetically kissing him on the nose. Not even on the furry bit, but on the damp blob at the end of it.

Angel said, "Yuck!" And then, as Rags began whopping his tongue lovingly over Melia's face: "Mum, that is gross!"

"Yes. Frankie, don't let him do that," said Mum. "It's not hygienic."

I let Rags lick my face all the time. But I have to admit I never kiss him on the damp blobby bit at the end of his nose; even I draw the line at that. I always kiss him on his fur.

"Rags, Rags, raggedy Rags," chanted Melia, taking Rags' front paws in her hands and doing a heavy stomping sort of jig round the kitchen.

"Raggedy raggedy," she chanted, crashing into Angel.

If I'd crashed into Angel, she would have shrieked at me. As it was Melia, she just gave a rather sickly smile and said, "I'm going upstairs... to the *tip*."

Melia stopped stomping and said, "What's the tip?"

"Her *bedroom*," snapped Angel. "That *I'm* having to sleep in!"

"Angel – Frankie – that dog—" Mum was beginning to sound a bit frayed at the edges. She patted Melia on the shoulder and said, "It's all right, you don't have to take any notice of Angel."

"No, cos she's loopy," I said. "Nobody takes any notice of her. Let's go in the garden and play with Rags."

Normally when I take Rags into the garden Mum calls after me to "Keep that dog out of my flower beds!" but today I think probably she was glad to get rid of him and Melia banging about the kitchen.

"Look," I said to Melia, "this is his favourite toy." It was a big orange football that he'd found over the park and insisted on carrying home with him. It must have had a small hole in it somewhere cos it kept shrinking and then puffing itself up again. Rags liked to squish it and squash it and nose it round the garden.

"Kick it for him," I said. "Rags, put it down for Melia... now, go on, kick it!"

WALLOP, went Melia. WHUMPF, went the ball.

Right into the middle of one of Mum's flower beds. Rags immediately went plunging after it. Fortunately there's not a lot of stuff to trample on at the beginning of January, but he still managed to scatter a load of pots in all directions. Melia giggled. I said, "Actually, he's not supposed to run across the flower beds." Her face fell, so then of course I felt bad and had to reassure her that it wasn't her fault.

"You weren't to know."

All the same I didn't quite see how she'd managed to do it, considering I'd gone to the trouble of making sure she was pointing in *exactly* the opposite direction. I couldn't have done it if I'd tried.

Rags had picked up the ball and was running about, shaking it.

"Chase him," I said. "That's what he wants you to do."

Melia obligingly set off in pursuit, shrieking

and giggling and crying, "Rags, come here, Rags!" She had a bit of a clumsy sort of run, with her feet splaying out and her arms going round like windmills. Rags thought it was a great game.

While I was collecting up the scattered flower pots, my phone rang. It was Jem, eager to know if Melia had arrived.

"Yes," I said. "We're in the garden, playing with Rags."

"What's she like? Is it going to be OK?"

"No problem." I turned to watch as Rags came bounding back, wild-eyed down the path, with Melia shrieking and clomping after him. "She's really good with Rags," I said. "And she does what she's told," I added.

Jem said, "Really?"

I said, "Yes. You just have to ask her, and she does it."

"Wow."

"Well, it certainly makes a nice change."

I paused, to let the words sink in. Only last week I'd had reason to ask Jem *very nicely* to stop banging her feet against the back of my chair and she'd been positively hostile. She'd accused me of being a nag and said she was sick of being bossed around. We'd almost fallen out over it.

"I guess it's just as well," said Jem. "I mean, if you've got to be responsible for her. You wouldn't want her arguing all the time."

"No," I said, "cos that's really annoying, when people do that."

Out of the corner of my eye, I saw Rags disappearing into some bushes at the far end of the garden and Melia floundering up the side of the compost heap.

"D'you want to speak to her?" I said to Jem. "Hey, Melia!" I waved at her. "Come and say hello!"

Obediently, Melia heaved herself out of the

compost heap and lumbered back down the garden. I held out the phone.

"Say hello to Jem."

Melia took the phone and bellowed into it: "Hello, Jem! I'm Melia."

"You'll see her tomorrow," I said. I took the phone back. "Gotta go. Melia's covered in compost!"

Later, when we went up to bed, Mum said, "Now, you girls, I don't want you lying awake talking half the night. It's a school day tomorrow. So into bed, lights out, and straight to sleep. Right?"

Melia said, "Right." She put a finger to her lips. "No talking!"

"You've got it," said Mum. "And that means you too, Frankie. Rags, are you going to stay downstairs?"

"Mum, no," I said. "He always sleeps with me!"

Sometimes he sleeps on the floor, and sometimes he sleeps on the bed. Sometimes, in the depths of winter, he even tries to sleep *in* the bed. But mostly he lies on top, taking up far more than his fair share of the duvet and grumbling whenever I turn over. To be honest, it's not really what I'd call comfortable, but I'm used to it by now. It wouldn't feel right, sleeping without Rags.

Mum muttered something about "dogs' hairs all over the place" and Rags galloped upstairs with me as usual.

"No talking," said Melia, as she got into her nightie.

She said it again as she got into bed. And then again as I turned off the light. And then again as she lay down. After that there was silence for a bit. All I could hear was the sound of Rags contentedly huffing and scrabbling as he settled himself on top of the duvet. And then, through the darkness, came a whisper: "Rags! D'you want to come and sleep with me?"

"He sleeps with me," I said.

Melia heaved a sigh. I wondered if she was missing her mum and if maybe I ought to tell her that she could have Rags, just for the one night. But I couldn't bring myself to do it. He was my dog, and he slept with me! I was really pleased when he showed no signs of moving. I reached out a hand and gave him a pat.

"Good boy!"

I think then I must have fallen asleep, cos the next thing I remember there was a thump as Rags jumped off the bed and I heard the sound of whispering and rustling.

"What are you doing?" I shot up the bed and switched the light back on. Both Rags and Melia started, guiltily. "What are you giving him? You're not giving him *chocolate*?"

I sprang out of bed and snatched a half-eaten bar of KitKat out of Melia's hand.

"Chocolate's poisonous to dogs! It can kill them!"

Tears of fright sprang into Melia's eyes.

"Don't ever, *ever*," I said, "give chocolate to dogs. Not *ever*!"

"I'm sorry," said Melia. The tears welled over and rolled down her cheeks. "I'm sorry, I'm sorry, I'm sorry, I'm s—"

"Just don't ever do it again," I said.

"I won't, I won't, I won't, I w—"

"*Ever.*"

"I promise, I p—"

"Sh!" I grabbed Rags and hauled him back on to my bed. "No talking. Mum said!"

She put a finger to her lips. "No talking. No talking! N—"

"That means QUIET," I said. "Go to sleep!"

Melia fell asleep almost immediately; I could

hear her making little whiffling noises. I stayed awake for hours. Rags spent the entire night crammed up close, with his head next to mine and his whiskers all stiff and prickly against my cheek. Really uncomfortable! But I was just so thankful I'd managed to stop Melia feeding him chocolate.

CHAPTER FOUR

"Now, don't forget," said Mum, as she saw me and Melia off to school next morning, "you're picking Emilia up at three thirty. Right?"

I said, *"Right."*

"Emilia, Frankie's going to come and collect you at the end of school, so you just wait there for her. Don't try coming home by yourself. I want you to come with Frankie."

"Come with Frankie." Melia nodded. "Wait there for her."

"That's it! Good girl. Frankie, just make sure you're there."

I said, "Mum, we've already agreed!" We'd been over and over it. "I already *said*."

"Well, I'm just reminding you. It's Emilia's first day, we don't want anything going wrong."

"*Mu-uum!*"

I did think she might have a bit more faith in me. All I had to do was collect Melia from school and bring her back home. Nothing to it! I'd been taking Rags up the park by myself since I was eight years old. At least Melia wasn't likely to go running off, or getting into punch-ups, or rolling in fox poo.

"OK, OK!" Mum held up her hands. "Enough! I've said my piece. Off you go, see you later."

"See you later, lallagator!"

Melia chanted it as we walked up the road.

I wondered whether to tell her that the word was alligator, not lallagator, but decided it wasn't really important.

"Look," I said, "there's Jemma and Skye." They were waiting for us on the corner. More often than not, it's me and Skye waiting for Jem, with Skye threatening to go on without her. Curiosity had obviously got Jem out of the house on time for once. "Skye's the tall one," I told Melia, "Jem's the little one." Tall and skinny: small and bubbly. "Jem's the one you spoke to on the phone."

Melia beamed her big banana beam and went gambolling up to them, hand at the ready.

"HELLO, SKYE! HELLO, JEM! I'M MELIA!"

The words came out in her normal bellow. A couple of girls on the other side of the road turned to see what was going on. One of them was Daisy Hooper, who is in our class. Trust her to be passing by at exactly the wrong moment! Not that I was ashamed or anything, but Daisy Hooper is the sort of girl who likes to store things up. I could see her clocking Melia, wondering who she was.

Jem, who is never fazed by anything, simply giggled and said, "Hi, Melia!"

"*HI!*" shouted Melia.

Skye sent me a worried look.

"It's all right," I said. "She's just happy. I've got to drop her off at St Giles and pick her up again later. Hey!" I dug Jem in the ribs. "Did you do your maths homework?"

"Did what I could," said Jem.

"I couldn't do *any* of it!"

"That's cos you weren't paying attention in class," said Skye.

I said, "I was paying attention!" I just don't have the sort of brain that can cope with numbers. They whizz about inside my head, all mad and shrieking. "It's all right for you," I grumbled. "You're like some kind of machine."

"I pay attention," said Skye. "I *listen*."

That may have been true. It was still an extremely irritating sort of thing to say.

"Honestly," I wailed at Jem, "I only managed to answer half a question!"

"I did three." Jem announced it, proudly. "Look!" She dived into her bag and pulled out her maths book.

"Let's see," said Skye. "See what you've got. Hm..." She frowned. "No. 1's wrong, for a start. So's no. 2! And no. 3. They're all wrong! I think you must have gone and added instead of taking away, or something. They don't bear *any resemblance* to the right answers!"

"Oh, well." Jem took her book back. She didn't seem bothered. "At least I tried. I ought to get marks for that."

"I *tried*," I said. "I just—"

"Hang about!" Skye suddenly stopped. "What's she doing?"

Omigod. We'd forgotten about Melia; we'd all gone walking on, leaving her to trail behind. She seemed to be playing some kind of game, jumping on and off the kerb, chanting to herself.

"*Up... dow... nup... dow... nup...*"

"Stop her," said Skye.

"Melia!" I yelled at her, but she took no notice.

"*Nup... dow...*"

"Like, she really does as she's told," marvelled Jem. "Without any argument!"

I said, "She does, normally. *Melia!*"

"She'll get herself run over," said Skye.

I yelled again. "*MELIA!*"

This time she heard me. She looked up, wobbled, and went crashing slap bang into a woman who was walking past. The woman glared and snapped, "Do you mind? Just watch where you're going!"

"Oh, God, this is so embarrassing," said Skye.

I went marching back and clamped my arm through Melia's. "Don't *do* that!" I said.

She immediately looked crestfallen. "Sorry sorry sorry s—"

"Sh!" I put a finger to my lips. "You could have got run over! Then what would Mum say? She'd be really mad!"

"She'd tell me off?" Melia's lip quivered. I said, "No! I'd be the one she told off. And that wouldn't be fair, would it?"

Slowly, Melia shook her head, waving it from side to side. *Left*... right. *Left*... right.

"It's OK," I said. "No one's mad at you." Still holding her by the arm, I hustled her back to join the others. "Let's hurry or you'll be late for school." I nearly added, "You wouldn't want that, would you?" but just in time I bit the words back. It might have started her on her head-waving again. I was already learning that once she got going on something she found it almost impossible to stop.

St Giles is a bit further on down the road from our school, but we all walked there together, even Skye, though I think secretly she would have preferred to let me and Jem go by ourselves. Melia had quickly recovered from being yelled at. As we left her at the entrance to the playground, she waved at us, windmilling with both arms, crying, "See you later, lallagator!"

"Yeah," I see. "Three thirty."

We turned, and headed back up the road.

Skye said, "Well."

There was a silence.

"It's only four weeks," I said.

Lots of things happened at school that day. Sometimes you have days when you just drift about from class to class in a kind of dream, so that when you get home and your mum says "How was school?" you have to think really hard to remember that you've even been there. Other times, life is just crammed with incidents. This was one of *those* times, which was why, later on – well! It's why the thing happened. My mind was full. I'm not trying to make excuses; just explain.

The first incident occurred in second period, which was maths with Mr Hargreaves. He had decided that we were all to mark our own homework, which I reckoned was a bit of a cheek considering he is the teacher and marking homework is part of what he is being paid for. If he'd taken it away like he usually did it would at least have postponed the moment of discovery. The fact that I'd only answered half a question...

I would have liked to have had a discussion about it. "Why should pupils be expected to mark their own work?" After all, these things are important, they are all part of politics, and we are supposed to take an interest in politics. I did put up my hand and suggest that marking our own work might not be such a good idea since it could encourage people to cheat, but Mr Hargreaves just gave a short sharp bark of rather threatening laughter and said he would like to see anyone try.

"You needn't think you can just write down the correct answers and give yourself full marks... I shall need proof of how you got them."

Glancing over Skye's shoulder, I saw that she had not only written down her answers but had shown all the working out, a whole page and a half of neat figures with plus signs and minus signs, not to mention signs for a load of other stuff which I didn't properly understand.

I sat dismally watching as she placed a small red tick by the side of every question. Jem had given up and was drawing faces on the cover of her maths book. They were always the same face: cheekbones you could slice bread with, enormous eyes, and long swishy hair. Jem has this dream that one day she will become a model. She is pretty enough, but what Mum calls 'pint-sized', meaning that if she went wandering into a field of long grass she would simply disappear from sight. Most models seem to be about 10 feet tall.

Skye is tall, and she is also skinny, but I am not quite sure she is pretty enough. In any case, she has far loftier ambitions such as, for instance, becoming prime minister. Well, that is what she once said, when a visitor at primary school asked her what she wanted to do when she grew up. She was only six at the time, so everyone thought it quite funny. But it wouldn't surprise me. "The British Prime Minister, Skye Samuels." She is bossy enough! And of course she is clever. When Mr Hargreaves asked if anyone had got full marks, hers was the only hand that went up.

Daisy Hooper groaned and rolled her eyes, but Daisy Hooper is our sworn enemy and suffers from torrents of raging jealousy. Most people just accept that Skye is some kind of boffin brain and automatically expect her to get full marks.

I must say I was a bit annoyed when Daisy claimed to have scored five. I looked at her through narrowed eyes, trying to assess whether she had found some foolproof method of cheating. I wouldn't put it past her.

Me and Jem were the only two people, apart from Cara Thompson, who didn't get any marks at all. Cara had been away at the start of term, so she had an excuse. Me and Jem didn't, apparently. That was what Mr Hargreaves said.

"Simply no excuse! I've told you over and

over, till I'm blue in the face... if you don't understand something, let me know! Don't just sit there like puddings, in some kind of mindless fog."

Daisy slewed round in her desk and gazed at us with an air of satisfaction. She just loves to gloat.

Mr Hargreaves, meanwhile, went on at some length. I have noticed, with teachers, that once they get on one of their hobby horses they seem unable to get off. They lash themselves up into a state. They say things that are really, in my opinion, quite uncalled for, such as, "Do you actually take *pleasure* in upsetting me?"

Daisy smirked. Skye, sitting stiff and straight between me and Jem, was obviously trying to pretend she didn't know us. Jem was putting the finishing touches to one of her faces, giving it big pouty lips and eyelashes like spiders' legs.

"*Well?*" roared Mr Hargreaves.

I jumped. It is just as well I don't have a weak heart.

"What do you have to say for yourselves?"

Jem muttered that she was sorry. I explained, very earnestly, that I hadn't liked to interrupt.

"Whaddya mean," bawled Mr Hargreaves, "you didn't like to interrupt?"

"When you were talking," I said. "You talked the whole lesson. It's rude to interrupt when people are talking."

Mr Hargreaves breathed, very deeply. I watched his face turn from red to purple. Daisy spun round again, to study me.

"Frankie Foster..." The words came out between clenched teeth. "If ever I have an apoplexy, you will be the cause of it!"

It wasn't a good start to the day.

Later on, in English, Miss Rolfe said she wanted to test our use of language. We were all to write a short paragraph describing the person sitting next to us.

"I want more than just lists... brown hair, blue eyes, that sort of thing. Be imaginative!"

I snatched up my pen, quite eagerly. Unlike numbers, which swarm inside my head like hordes of angry wasps, words are more orderly. They line themselves up in ranks, waiting to be chosen. And I do think I have quite a good imagination.

"What are you saying about me?" Skye craned over to look. I shoved her away.

"Gerroff!"

"Are you being rude?"

"I'm being *imaginative.*"

"Well, then, so am I," said Skye.

This is what I wrote about her: "Skye has long hair the colour of hay. It is wispy, like a shredded net curtain. She is tall as a tree, and thin as a pin, with legs like stilts. Her eyes are grey like the sky when it is full of rain clouds, and her nose is a pointed pencil. Her mouth is a small 0 with two rows of perfect ivory stumps."

This is what Skye wrote about me: "She has a round face, snubby-nosed and covered in blotches. Her mouth stretches wide like an elastic band with large strong teeth like a horse. Her eyes are round as marbles, to match her face. They are faintly blue in colour. Shapewise, she is rather like a box, with arms and legs sticking out at the corners. Her arms are covered in blotches like her face, and her legs are what some people call sturdy and some call tree trunks. She likes to play hockey, and they are very good legs for that."

"*Blotches?*" I shrieked, as we stood in line with our trays at lunch time.

"Freckles," said Skye.

"Then why didn't you say so?"

"I was being imaginative! And anyway, what about this?" She delved into her bag and pulled out her rough book. She'd actually made notes! *Wispy, like a shredded net curtain*... thank you very much! And what are you sniggering about?" She turned accusingly on Jem.

"It's funny," said Jem. "Like you saying Frankie was shaped like a box."

"Well, she is!"

"Yes, and you're thin as a pin," I said.

"With legs like stilts." Jem gave a happy cackle and left the lunch queue to do a stilt-like prance up and down. "And Frankie's –" she began on a heavy clump, clomp – "are tree trunks!"

We both turned our backs on her.

"Is my nose really like a pointed pencil?" said Skye.

"I just meant it was noble," I pleaded. "Not snubby, like mine."

"That wasn't meant as an insult." Skye was

quick to assure me. "You have a sweet little nose! Sort of... tilted."

"Yes, and you have nice teeth."

"You said they were stumps!"

"I couldn't think what else to call them. I did say they were perfect!"

"And I said you had good legs for playing hockey."

In the end, we forgave each other. It was Jem we couldn't forgive, with her foolish giggling.

"So rude," I grumbled. "Just because she's the pretty one."

Rhianna Shah had described Jem as looking like a "colourful wild flower". As Skye said, totally naff. To be fair to Jem, she didn't gloat over it, so that by the end of the afternoon, as we went down to the locker room to collect our coats, I was grudgingly prepared to accept her apology.

"It was just – you know! Kind of funny at the time," said Jem.

I pointed out that I didn't reckon she would find it very funny if someone said she had legs like tree trunks, at which she looked suitably ashamed and agreed that she probably wouldn't.

"But you did say Skye had legs like stilts."

"Stilts aren't as bad as tree trunks." Tree trunks are insulting.

"You said her nose was pointy!"

"She said mine was snubby. It isn't snubby, is it?" I turned anxiously to look in the nearest mirror. My nose looked back at me... *snubby*. "It is!" I wailed. "It's ridiculous!"

Some of the others crowded round, eager to offer their opinions.

"It's not so much snubby, as..."

"What, what?"

"Sort of..."

"Blobby?" suggested someone.

"Yeah, blobby! Like a blob."

"You could always try sleeping with a clothes

peg on it. I read about someone doing that."

"Did it work?"

"Dunno."

"What about plastic surgery? You could get a whole new nose if you had plastic surgery. You could choose whatever shape you wanted!"

"Don't think my mum'd let me."

"Some mums do. What about that one that gave her daughter a boob job for her birthday?"

"*Boob* job?"

"It was on the news. Twelve-year-old girl gets boob job."

The conversation surged on, taking me with it. I wasn't 'specially interested in boob jobs, seeing I had none to speak of, but I always like to hear about these things. It adds to one's store of knowledge.

It wasn't until Skye suddenly came clattering down the steps that something clicked in my brain.

"I thought you had a piano lesson?" I said.

"It's been cancelled. I thought you were going to pick up Melia?"

Melia. Omigod! What was the time?

"It's nearly twenty to four!" yelped Jem.

Panic-stricken, we galloped up the steps and across the yard. Skye, on her stilt-like legs, galloped with us. Me and my tree trunks forged ahead, pounding down the road with my heart hammering. Please let her be there, please let her be there, please please please!

But she wasn't. The school playground was empty. Not a sign of anyone.

"If you're looking for that daffy girl you were with—"

I spun round. Daisy Hooper was coming out of the newsagent with her friend Talia.

"She went wandering off. That way." Daisy flapped a hand. "Few minutes ago. Didn't look like she knew where she was going."

We all set off at a run. Melia was headed in totally the wrong direction. She was headed into town, towards the main road. Did she even know how to cope with main roads? Suppose she tried to cross over? How was I going to go back and admit to Mum that I'd completely forgotten about her?

"MELIA!" I shouted.

"There she is." Skye pointed. I recognised the blue uniform of St Giles and the slightly splay-footed walk of Melia. Oh, God, she was about to step into the road!

"Melia," I bellowed, "wait!"

We caught up with her just in time.

"Frankie!" she cried. She had tears rolling down her cheeks. "I got lost!"

"It's all right," I said, soothingly. "I'm here now. Let's go home!"

We all made a huge great fuss of her, even Skye, and took her into the newsagent to buy her some sweets and cheer her u

"Have whatever you want," I said.

Melia beamed and shouted, "Sticky Fingaz!"

Sticky Fingaz are these really gross sucky things made to look like human hands, except they are bright red, and gooey, and ooze all over the place. I grew out of them when I was about nine years old. Watching Melia slurp and chomp as she attacked each finger I began to have a bit of sympathy with Mum, who always claimed she couldn't bear to watch me eat them. It was a somewhat disgusting sight, but it made Melia happy.

Daisy was still lounging about outside. She made a loud splurging noise as we walked past. "I see you found her, then."

"Yes," I said. "Thank you."

Melia turned, and beamed a big squidgy beam in Daisy's direction.

"I got Sticky Fingaz!"

"Yeah, great, go for it," said Daisy.

"Snot face," I said, as we walked away.

I think Skye was quite relieved when we reached Sunnybrook Gardens and parted company. She is a bit more sensitive than me and Jem; she gets embarrassed quite easily. But she was very loyal, she didn't try to distance herself, like walking ahead or anything.

"See you tomorrow!" shouted Melia.

"Listen, it's probably best not to tell Mum about getting lost," I said as we made our way up the road. "It would only worry her. So we won't say anything. OK?"

"OK." Melia nodded. Up-down, up-down. She did everything so *vigorously*.

I was on tenterhooks as Mum demanded to know why we were so late.

"I was getting worried. You should have been here twenty minutes ago!"

Melia beamed. Her lips, and her tongue, and

even her teeth were stained bright red. She'd consumed almost the entire hand; she just had one knuckle left.

"Frankie bought me Sticky Fingaz," she said. "And we met this girl called Snot Face!"

Mum said, "*Snot* Face?"

"It's not her real name," I told Melia. "It's just what I call her."

"Snot Face!" Melia chuckled happily. She held out her last remaining knuckle. "Can I give to Rags?"

I was so grateful to her that I said yes. She had kept my secret so I reckoned she deserved to give Rags a treat. She was all right, was Melia!

CHAPTER
FIVE

Sometimes on a Saturday morning, if nothing else is happening, we like to go into the shopping centre and mooch round the shops. We don't usually buy anything as we don't usually have any money, but it's fun just to look. Dad finds it amusing. He says he imagines us pathetically standing there, with our noses pressed to the glass.

"Watching all the rich people inside!"

I have tried pointing out that if I got a bit more pocket money I wouldn't have to stand with my nose pressed to any glass, but Dad says, "Go on! You enjoy it."

It's true, we do. We have these games that we play, like the Wedding Game, when we pick out our favourite wedding dresses; and the Ugliest Outfit on Earth game, when we giggle our way round the fashion department at Turton's, pointing at stuff we think is hideous and going, "Yeeurgh! Imagine being seen in that!" You have to be careful as the ladies in the fashion department are rather snooty and posh, and they don't always like you giggling and pointing. It's probably just as well we have Skye to keep us in order. She says that left to ourselves me and Jem would go completely over the top. She could be right! We do tend to egg each other on.

We'd made arrangements that Saturday to

meet up at 11 o'clock in our usual place. I'd thought it was just going to be the three of us, but Mum assumed automatically that we were taking Melia.

"To the shopping centre?" I said.

"Why not? She'd love it!"

I said, "Yes, but..."

"But what?" said Mum. "Don't tell me you're getting tired of her already!"

"It's not that," I said. It wasn't that I was *tired* of her. I mean, she was really sweet and obliging, and after all she had kept quiet about me forgetting to pick her up. But she'd been with us for nearly a week now, and I'd learnt that you really did have to watch her the entire time for fear she'd go wandering off in the wrong direction, or strike up a conversation with total strangers. Even *go* with total strangers.

"You know, Frankie, I did warn you," said Mum.

"Yes," I said, "I know! It's just –" I waved a hand. "The others."

"Jemma and Skye? Oh, come on, I'm sure between the three of you you can manage all right! Or are you saying they're tired of her?"

"N-no. Not exactly."

Just that it wasn't the same, with Melia tagging along. I didn't think Jem would mind; I wasn't so sure about Skye. Twice in the past few days she'd made excuses not to walk home with us. But I had promised Mum. She was relying on me! And I did owe Melia.

"It would make her so happy," said Mum. "And it would help me out. I have two of my ladies coming this morning for fittings."

What she meant was she couldn't watch over Melia and see to her ladies at the same time. You just never knew with Melia what she was going to get up to. She might even open the front door and let Rags go rushing out. I had this vision of him joyously galloping up to the park by himself. Running across the road, straight under the wheels of a car... it made me go quite weak and watery just thinking of it. You had to watch out for Rags just as you did for Melia. It was that that decided me: I told Mum that I would take her. Anything rather than Rags being run over.

Melia's face lit up with one of her big beams when she heard the news.

"Shopping centre! Shopping centre!" She held Rags' front paws and they danced up and down together. "We're going to the shopping centre!"

"Not with Rags," said Mum.

"Not Rags?" Her beam faded. She loved Rags; she always wanted to include him in everything. She'd have taken him to school with her if she could. "Put him onna lead?" she pleaded.

"Not in the shopping centre. They don't like dogs in there."

"Mm." Melia nodded, wisely. "I suppose in case he does a whoopsie. People might walk in it! Ugh, yuck! I walked in one, once. I got it *all over*. Pooh, pooh!" She held her nose. "What a pong! W—"

"Yes, well, this is it," said Mum. "You can't be too careful. Off you go now!" She gave me this little encouraging smile as she held open the front door. "Have a good time!"

I could see at once, from the look on Skye's face, that she hadn't been expecting me to bring Melia. Melia bawled, "HELLO, SKYE!" at the top of her voice, as usual. Skye said, "Yeah, hi," and gave me this agonised look.

"I couldn't help it," I hissed. "Mum's got fittings all morning."

"What about your dad? Isn't he there?"

"Dad's working."

Jem appeared at this point, and Melia went lolloping off to meet her.

"Hello, Jem! We're going to the shopping centre!"

"We've had her all week," said Skye. "Couldn't one of the others take a turn?"

I had to remind her that I was the one who'd originally offered to be responsible. Right from the start Angel had made it clear she wasn't going to get involved.

"And Tom's worse than useless."

Even Skye couldn't argue with that.

"Melia'll be OK," I said. I said it as much to convince myself as to convince Skye. "So long as we just remember to keep an eye on her."

It would have been all right if we hadn't gone into the China & Glass department of Turton's. We never go into the China & Glass department! It was Skye's fault; she was the one that took us there. She said she wanted to look for something for her nan's birthday present. She wasn't going to *buy* anything; she just wanted to see what was on offer. But it obviously wasn't a sensible place to take Melia.

We did our best to keep an eye on her. We kept *all* our eyes on her. We didn't relax for a minute, hardly. You couldn't with Melia. Wherever we went, she wanted to finger things. She kept snatching stuff up and shouting, "Hey, Frankie! Want one of these? Jem, Jem, how about this?"

If she wasn't touching, she was knocking things over. I mean, she didn't even *need* to touch. All she had to do was just breathe and things went toppling down. Like we were walking past this stand with really expensive glasses, all sparkly like diamonds. Jem was telling us about her guinea pig, how she'd thought she'd lost him.

"Honestly, we hunted *everywhere*. And then, guess what? Mum found him, all curled up in her –" she lowered her voice – "her *underwear* drawer!"

So, yes, OK, me and Skye had been listening to the underwear story, but out of the corner of my eye I was still watching Melia. *I* didn't know she was going to make a sudden dart. How was I to know? I'm not a mind reader! In any case, Melia's mind was really muddled. It was that that made her behaviour so unpredictable.

The first I knew was when she reached out a hand and crooned, "Ooh! Lovely glasses!" And before we realised what was happening one of them went bouncing to the floor. Thank goodness it was soft carpet! Cos those glasses, they cost £15 each. *£15!* Just for a glass.

This really snotty woman came rushing over. Boy, was she ratty! She told us we ought to know better than to go round touching things.

"We weren't touching," I said. I'd seen Melia's hand; it hadn't even *reached* the glasses. "We were just looking."

"Well, don't!" snapped the woman.

We felt really humiliated. Nothing like that had ever happened to us before! And anyway, it wasn't fair to put the blame on us. We'd already told Melia not to touch; we couldn't very well tell her not to *look*. Or to stop breathing. Cos I reckoned it was the breathing that had done it. Breathing too heavily and creating a draught. They obviously couldn't have stacked their glasses very well if just a little bit of breath could upset them.

We got out as fast as we could. It was Skye who led the charge, racing ahead like a daddy long legs with Jem whizzing in hot pursuit and me dragging Melia by the arm. Even though I had hold of her, she still managed to crash into a display stand and knock a bunch of hats to the floor, and then, just to make matters worse, almost trample on one.

"I thought you were going to keep an eye on her?" panted Skye.

I said, "I am! But she moves too fast."

We decided it would probably be best if we left Turton's altogether and went somewhere else.

"Somewhere she can't break stuff."

It was Jem who suggested the HMV shop. "Go and have a look round."

"Can I touch?" said Melia.

I said, "Yes, but only if you put things back where you got them."

"*That's* a mistake," said Skye.

Big mistake. We shouldn't ever have told Melia she could touch things. Before we know it, it's all gone to her head and she's snatching up CDs, one after another, crying, "Frankie, do you like the *Pink Crystals*? Jem, do you like *Groove*? Do you like *Voice Over*? Do you like *Scream*?" Shouting out the names of these bands, really loud for everyone to hear, so that all over the shop people are looking at us and sniggering, and Skye's like, "Omigod, does she have to?"

Jem's got a fit of the giggles and Melia obviously thinks she's impressing people cos she starts on this pretend swooning and fainting when she finds one of her favourites.

"Pieter Kruger! Yum yum!" She's pressing the CD to her lips and making slobbery kissy noises over it. "Yummy yummy yummy, y—"

Skye makes a strangulated yelping sound and bolts for the exit. I grab the CD and stuff it back into the rack, then seize hold of Melia and march her out, followed by Jem, still giggling.

"Well, I'm glad *someone* finds it funny," hissed Skye.

By now it wasn't just Jem who was giggling but Melia too, except that she wasn't so much giggling as giving these great swooping cackles like something out of a comic strip. *Hoo hoo hoo!* I don't think she really knew what she was laughing at; she just wanted to join in with Jem. Skye tutted, impatiently.

"Your face," choked Jem. She contorted her features into a mad grimace, her teeth bared and her lips pulled back. "If you could have seen it!"

Skye doesn't like to be laughed at. I don't suppose anyone does. But it is worse for somebody like Skye, who is always so serious and tries so hard to be dignified.

"This is a *disaster*," she said.

"Oh, I dunno," said Jem, "I think it's quite fun! You're having fun, aren't you?"

She nudged at Melia, and Melia beamed proudly. I guess she thought she was pleasing us.

"Let's just *go*," said Skye.

I said, "What, you mean go home?"

She looked at me, long and hard. "What else would you suggest?"

Jem giggled again. "We could always go into Smith's and let Melia trash the magazines."

"Yes, yes!" Melia clapped her hands. "Go into Smith's! Go into Smith's!"

"No, thank *you*," said Skye.

I thought she was probably right, and that it might be best to take Melia back home. I wasn't honestly sure how much more my nerves could stand.

"Mind you, we shouldn't ever have been in China and Glass in the first place," I said. "Might have known she'd knock something over."

Skye stopped. She put her hands on her hips.

"Are you saying it was my fault?"

"I'm just *saying*. I don't even know what we were doing there! Wasn't like you bought anything."

"Hey, hey!" Before me and Skye could fall out, Jem had come prancing up, with Melia in tow. "Let's go into Boots and try out lipsticks!"

It was one of our favourite pastimes, going into Boots and sampling the cosmetics. I was tempted, in spite of myself. It seemed a bit of a waste, being in the shopping centre and *not* going into Boots.

"Oh, come on!" said Jem. "There's nothing she can break."

"Famous last words," muttered Skye.

Well, she didn't break anything. She didn't knock anything over. She didn't start shouting and draw attention to herself. In fact, to be honest, we kind of forgot about her for a few minutes. It was almost like it was just the three of us, same as usual. And then I said, "Oh, God, where's Melia?" and we all started flying about in a panic. We found her happily standing in front of a mirror with a tube of lipstick in her hand. She'd gone mad and plastered herself! Bright green eye shadow, with cheeks like big red beach balls and eyelashes sticking out in spider's legs, stiff with mascara. She'd painted her eyebrows soot black, two furry caterpillars crawling across her brow, and was busy coating her lips with purple lipstick. I snatched it from her.

"That's not a tester!"

"Oh, God, oh, God," moaned Skye. "Put it back, quick, before someone sees!"

We bundled out, in a panic – and then immediately began to worry in case we might have been caught on camera.

"It's theft," said Skye. "We could be done!"

"You were the one that said put it back," said Jem.

"You were the one that said go in there!"

"Yeah, well, so? You didn't have to come! You could have stayed outside."

"I would have if I'd known she was going to start stealing stuff!"

"Maybe we should go back and, like... pay for it?" I said.

"Don't see why *we* should have to pay for it," said Jem. "She's your responsibility."

"Oh, for goodness' sake!" snapped Skye. "Let's just go and get it over with."

Nervously, we crept back into the store. I was expecting any moment a hand to descend on my shoulder. I felt like a criminal! I *was* a criminal. We had to get to that lipstick immediately and pay for it!

Fortunately it wasn't one of the expensive brands, but all the same I was grateful when Skye insisted on paying half. The lady who took our money was worried cos she said the lipstick had been opened. I told her that was all right.

"Our friend did it and that's why we're buying it."

The lady took one look at Melia and said, "Ah. Right. I see."

"That was taking a chance," hissed Jem, as we got back outside. "She could have called the p'lice!"

"Oh, shut up," I said. "What shall we do with the horrible thing?" I mean, who wants to wear purple lipstick? Skye said chuck it in the bin. It was Jem, who hadn't even helped pay for it, who said give it to Melia. Melia's big clown face, with its purple lips, broke into a delighted beam. A frightening sight! She hadn't just got purple lips, she'd got purple teeth, as well. I wondered if we should take her back to Turton's and into the Ladies and scrub her clean, but Skye, sounding a bit hysterical, said, "Let's just *go*." So we went.

Me and Skye walked ahead, leaving Jem to trail behind with Melia. Considering she hadn't even offered to pay her share of the lipstick, I didn't feel too guilty.

"After all," as I said to Skye, "it was her idea, going into Boots. *We'd* already decided to go home. And omigod," I wailed, "look what's coming!"

Skye said, "What, what?"

Daisy Hooper, that was what. That girl had a positive knack for turning up where she was least wanted. She was standing outside McDonald's and there just was no way of avoiding her. Me and Skye did our best. Determinedly we marched past with our noses in the air, pretending not to notice. And then I heard Melia's happy cry: "HELLO, SNOT FACE!"

Frankly, I just wanted the ground to burst open and swallow me up. It is one thing to refer to your enemy by a rude name behind her back; quite another to do it in front of her. As Skye said, "That's really gone and blown it." She'd know for sure where Melia had got it from.

"Oh, who cares?" Jem skipped after us, defiantly dragging Melia by the hand. "She's just a ratbag, anyway!"

"I *told* her," I said. "Melia, I told you! Snot Face isn't her real name. You're not supposed to *call* her that."

By the time we arrived home I was feeling quite frazzled. Mum said, "Well, Emilia looks as though she's enjoyed herself! How did it go? Not so bad, was it?"

Crossly I said, "Don't ask! I'm going to take Rags out, and I'm going by myself."

I'd had enough responsibility for one morning.

CHAPTER SIX

It was Melia who broke Tom's science project. I'd seen her earlier, touching at it. I *told* her not to.

"He hates people interfering with his stuff."

He's not like Angel, who goes up in a puff of smoke if you even just look at things, but he can get quite snakey if you mess with one of his projects. I did warn her. What more was I supposed to do? He shouldn't have brought it downstairs in the first place, let alone leave it on a low table, where she could get at it.

I could see that it fascinated her. It was bristling with little glass tubes, and different-coloured wires, and it kept making this buzzing sound. Melia had discovered that by jiggling some of the wires she could make the buzz turn into a whine, and if she put a finger over the end of a tube she could make it pop and whistle.

"You better hadn't keep doing that," I said.

Even as I said it, her hand had gone reaching out again. She was like Rags, when he got obsessed with something. Like once when one of his dog biscuits rolled under the fridge, and Rags knew that it was there even though nobody else did. He could obviously smell it. He lay on his side on the floor for ages, frantically scraping with his paws and making squealing noises, until in the end Mum said it was driving her mad and she told Tom to, "Get down there and shine a torch under the fridge and see what his problem is," and there was the biscuit, right at the back. Tom had to use a length of cane from the garden to poke it out.

Rags was happy once he'd got his biscuit. I had the feeling Melia wouldn't be happy till she'd succeeded in pulling out some of the wires and tubes. You could tell she was just itching to have a go. I *knew* she couldn't be trusted! But I didn't see why I should be expected to keep an eye on her every single minute of every day. I had to have *some* time to myself. It was only yesterday we'd been on our disastrous trip to the shopping centre; I reckoned I deserved a bit of a break from looking after Melia. I mean, the rest of the family surely had to do something?

Mum was in the front room with one of her

ladies. Tom was upstairs on his computer. Dad was working. Angel, on the other hand, wasn't doing anything; not as far as I could see. Just lounging about in the kitchen, painting her nails with silver nail polish.

"Look," I said to Melia, "there's Angel, painting her nails. Maybe she'd let you paint yours if you asked her nicely." Then I shoved her into the kitchen and raced upstairs to get a bit of homework done in peace and quiet.

Homework is not exactly my idea of fun, but it seems life is full of boring, time-wasting stuff that you are forced to do if you want to stay out of trouble. Dad says it is good for the soul. I can't see it myself; I'm sure my soul would be far better off *without* all the aggravation. But the shadow of Mr Hargreaves was hanging over me, so I reckoned I'd better at least make an attempt at doing some of his horrible maths homework.

When I went back downstairs at lunch time Mum was still in the front room, Tom, as far as I knew, was still sitting at his computer, and Angel had vanished. I found Melia in the kitchen on her own, sitting with Rags in his dog bed.

"Did you paint your nails?" I said.

Melia shook her head. She seemed a bit down.

"Did you ask her?"

"She wouldn't let me."

"Well, really!" I felt quite exasperated. How mean could you get? Angel appeared at that moment, her nails all gleaming silver. "You might have let Melia have a go!" I said.

Angel tossed her head. "Don't see why I should let her use my stuff. Let her use yours."

"I don't have any! I don't paint my nails."

"Hardly could," said Angel, "state they're in. Nothing there to paint."

It's true my nails are a bit stubby. That is

because in moments of stress I tend to bite them. I have a *lot* of stress in my life, what with people like Mr Hargreaves bellowing and bawling, and Mum nagging at me to tidy my bedroom, put things away after me, pick my clothes up off the floor, I mean the list just goes on and on. It is all STRESS. Little did I know that more was about to descend on me...

It came in the shape of Tom, crashing furiously through the kitchen door.

"Who's been messing with my science project? Was it you?"

He glared at me, his eyes popping. I retreated, hastily, behind the kitchen table. I am quite accustomed to Angel being in a rage, she practically lives in one; but Tom almost never gets mad. As a rule he is just, like, totally unflappable. Dad once said that if you told him an asteroid was about to collide with the planet and wipe us all out, he would just grunt, "Uh?"

So on the rare occasions when he does blow up, it can be quite scary.

"It *was* you." He advanced upon me, round the table. "I know it was you!"

"It's always her," said Angel.

I opened my mouth to protest: "I haven't been anywhere near your rotten science project!" But then I caught sight of Melia, crouched in the dog bed, trembling, with both arms wrapped tightly round Rags as if for protection, and the words froze on my lips. All that came out was a small, stifled squawk.

"Just admit it!" roared Tom.

I swallowed. Melia looked up at me, beseechingly.

"What's going on?" Mum had come in. "I feel tension! Who's done what, and why?"

Angel pointed silently at me.

Mum said, "Frankie? What have you been up to now?"

"She's only gone and ruined my science project." Tom said it bitterly. "Took me days to set up, that did."

"Shouldn't have left it on the table," I muttered.

"It was perfectly all right on there if you hadn't gone and touched it!"

"I didn't touch it!"

"So how come all the wires have been pulled out?"

Tom was shouting; he was really mad. I wanted so much to shout back at him, "It wasn't me, it was Melia!" But she'd crept out of the bed and her hand had stolen into mine. I could feel her shaking.

"Frankie, how did it happen?" said Mum.

Crossly I said, "I don't know! It was an accident. I was chasing Rags. He bumped into the table, and it all went on the floor."

Tom's eyes had narrowed. "That wouldn't

make the wires come out! Someone's been yanking at them."

"I haven't yanked at your manky wires! It was an accident."

"All right," said Mum, "all right. Let's try and calm down. Frankie, I think the least you can do is apologise to your brother. And Tom, can you put the wires back again?"

There was a moment's silence while we both brooded. Then somewhat grudgingly Tom said, "Well, yeah, I s'ppose... but it'll take all day!" I mumbled that I was sorry it had happened, and Mum suggested we all sat down and had some lunch.

"I do think," she added, "that it would be safer, Tom, if you took your project back upstairs. That way, there can't be any more accidents."

Tom glowered. "If it was an accident."

"I said! It was!"

"Tom! Frankie!" Mum rapped on the kitchen table. "Please! I'm sorry it happened and I'm sorry it means more work for you, Tom, but Frankie has apologised, she can't do more. Let's stop, now, we're upsetting Emilia. It's all right, sweetheart!" Mum put an arm round Melia's shoulders and gave her a hug. "You're not the one that's in trouble."

You'd have thought, after that, Melia might have learnt her lesson. You'd have thought she might have been a bit careful what she did with her hands and feet. But if anything it just seemed to make her worse. Later that day, she broke Mum's favourite coffee mug. I watched her do it. I'd just made some coffee 'specially to take in to Mum, cos she was working so hard with all these ladies turning up and I like to do these little things occasionally, just to help out. Washing up, for instance, or vacuuming. I 'specially enjoy vacuuming. I used to enjoy ironing but I'm not allowed to do that any more, since one of Angel's blouses got shrivelled and everyone blamed me. I always get the blame for everything. It never even occurred to Tom, or to Mum, that it might have been Melia and not me that had pulled out Tom's wires. Oh, no! It had to be Frankie. But it was definitely Melia that broke Mum's mug.

I'd put it out on the table, ready to pour the water in, and even as I reached out for the kettle Melia had gone flumping past with her arms flailing about and sent it flying. She wasn't even aware that she'd done it! I stared, in disbelief. I just couldn't believe that she'd gone and broken it. I'd given that mug to Mum last year, on her birthday. I'd chosen it 'specially cos it was so pretty, I knew Mum would love it. It had all flowers painted on it, like the ones she grew in the garden. Pansies, I think they were.

Mum had been really pleased. She'd said,

"Oh, Frankie, that is quite beautiful! From
on, I shall make it my special coffee mug.
Everyone take note... this is the mug I have my
coffee in!"

Melia turned round. One of her feet went
scrunch. She looked down, in surprise.

"Frankie," she cried, "you've broken the mug!
Frankie, you're so *clumsy.*"

I am not an evil-tempered person, I really
am not. I don't fly into tremendous rages and
yell at people. But in that moment I felt like
getting hold of Melia and shaking her. I said,
"Listen, *goofball*!" and I gave her a poke. "How'm
I s'pposed to have done it? I wasn't anywhere
near! I was over there, wasn't I? By the stove."
Poke. "It was you! You were the—"

That was when she skidded on a bit of broken
mug and went down *flomp* on to the floor.

I might as well be honest. My immediate
reaction was to feel intensely irritated. Trust

Melia! And then Rags came wobbling over, with his tail wagging, and pushed his ball at her. He loves it when people are down at his level, he thinks they want to play.

It was Melia, not me, who pushed him to safety. "Rags, go 'way!" she cried. "You get hurt!"

For a moment, I almost softened. I mean, I'd yelled at her, I'd called her goofball, I'd pushed her over, and all she could think was that Rags might get hurt. But then I looked at the shattered pieces of Mum's broken mug, and all my anger rose up again and nearly choked me. I yanked Melia to her feet and shoved both her and Rags into the garden while I got the dustpan and brush and began sweeping up the bits. Angel came in while I was doing it.

"Oh," she said, "you've broken Mum's mug!"

"It wasn't me," I said. "It was Melia. She just walked past and it fell over." I sighed. "Mum loved her mug!"

"Hm, well... now you know how it feels," said Angel.

She didn't say it unkindly, she actually sounded quite sympathetic for once, but the fact is she has never really forgiven me for shrivelling her blouse. I wondered if I would ever forgive Melia for breaking Mum's mug.

I supposed I would have to; you can't go on nursing a grudge for ever. Not unless you're Angel, who tends to collect grudges the way other people collect shoes, or china ornaments. She stuffs them all into one big bag which she carries around with her wherever she goes. Dunno what she'll do when the bag gets filled; start on a second one, I guess.

I tried quite hard to go on feeling aggrieved. Mum had so loved her mug! But then this really hysterical thing happened and my grudge just melted away. We were downstairs, watching television; me, and Mum, and Dad. Melia was in the bath, Tom was in his room, still putting his wires back, Angel was in the hall, saying goodbye to her latest boyfriend (whose name I cannot now remember, she has had so many of them). Suddenly, the air was ripped apart by this bloodcurdling screech and what sounded like a herd of buffalo thundering down the stairs. Dad said, "What in heaven's name is going on?" and we all rushed out into the hall.

The thundering was Rags tearing down the stairs, with Melia, clutching a bath towel round herself, thumping after him.

"Rags stole my knickers!" shrieked Melia.

They were dangling from his mouth. As he reached the hall he rolled an eye at us and galloped off, shaking the knickers from side to side. Melia galloped in hot pursuit. Down the hall, up the hall, back up the stairs, back down the stairs, still clutching at her bath towel.

In the midst of all the noise and confusion,

Tom appeared on the landing. He didn't seem to notice anything peculiar going on. Very solemnly he informed us that he had put his wires back in – "It is functioning again" – before walking past Melia, in her bath towel, walking past Rags, with his knickers, and stomping off in silence to the kitchen.

For some reason, this cracked Mum up; and once Mum had cracked up, we all cracked up. I was giggling at Rags, who'd managed to get his head through one of the knicker legs and was now wearing them on top of his head like a bonnet. I guess that was what the boyfriend was laughing at too. He cried, "Go, Rags!" and made a snatch at the knickers as Rags wheeled past. Mum seemed to have been more amused by Tom. I don't know what Dad was amused by, Tom or Rags or both, but he was definitely laughing. Even Melia was laughing. Great squeals came bursting out of her, making her shake so much she almost lost control of her bath towel. Mum rushed and caught at it just in time.

The only one who didn't laugh was Angel. She stood by the front door, stiff with outrage, her lips all pursed and puckered like she was sucking on a lemon. She was embarrassed, I suppose, because of her boyfriend being there, though I really don't know what she had to be embarrassed about. They weren't her knickers. And Melia *was* covered in a towel. Well, more or less. The boyfriend wasn't embarrassed, but Angel likes to stand on her dignity. Plus she has *no* sense of humour.

I did find it difficult, though, after that, to go on feeling cross with Melia. She couldn't help being the way she was. She didn't mean to upset people, breaking things and knocking things over; it just happened. I suddenly felt generous. I decided to make a REALLY BIG sacrifice.

"Hey, Melia!" I said, as we went to bed that night.

She looked at me uncertainly, pulling up the duvet and stuffing a corner of it into her mouth.

"It's OK," I said. "I'm not mad at you! I was going to ask you something."

Melia went on munching at the duvet, her eyes big and apprehensive. She obviously didn't trust me. She thought I was some kind of horrible bully!

"I was wondering," I said, "whether you'd like Rags to sleep with you? Just for tonight! Just this once."

That got her going. She sprang up immediately, her face engulfed in a great beam.

"Frankie, Frankie, thank you, thank you!" Before I knew what she was doing she'd hurled herself at me and locked both arms round my neck. And then she hesitated, and in doubtful tones whispered, "Frankie, I didn't really break the mug, did I?"

I told her not to worry about it. "These things happen. Rags, you go and sleep with Melia! *Just for tonight.*"

I don't know how long he stayed with her, but when I woke up in the morning he was cuddled up next to me, as usual. He knew whose dog he was!

CHAPTER
SEVEN

The next day, at break, while Skye was having an extra music lesson to make up for the one she'd missed, me and Jem sat in the downstairs cloakroom, huddled together over one of the hot water pipes. We are not supposed to sit in the cloakroom, we are supposed to be outside even when it is ice cold and freezing, but just now and again we manage to sneak in undetected. There is hideous trouble, of course, if we are found, and if Skye had been with us we wouldn't have been doing it since Skye is one of those law-abiding people that think rules are there to be obeyed. Me and Jem are more, like, *some* rules are there to be obeyed; others are just stupid and pointless. Such as being made to go outside and freeze half to death. I couldn't help a slightly guilty feeling that it was a great deal more *comfortable* without Skye there to lecture us and nag.

"Look," I said, peering through one of the mesh-covered windows, "people are turning blue. Their lips are blue. And oh, look, there's Daisy! I do believe her knee caps are bouncing up and down."

Jem said, "Yeah." She seemed preoccupied. I watched for a while as she frowningly sorted a tube of Smarties into different colours.

"Green one," I said. I pointed. "Over there."

"Oh. Yeah." Absently, Jem picked up the green one and popped it into her mouth, thus breaking her own rule about not starting to eat until all the colours had been arranged in rows.

I turned back to the window. "People could die out there. Get frostbite and die. You know what happens if you get frostbite? You rot. All your fingers and toes drop off. And then it starts to creep up your legs. And it *smells*. Once that happens, you're doomed."

Jem said, "Yeah?" Then suddenly, cramming her mouth with a great fistful of Smarties, she gabbled, "Saddy meenskygobyernanprez."

Well, that was what it sounded like.

"You what?" I said.

Jem swallowed. "On Saturday me and Skye are going to go and buy her nan's birthday present."

I said, "You and Skye?"

"She wants to get that little flower thingie

we saw? The thing with primroses? Cos that's
what her nan's name is... Primrose."

"Yes," I said, "I know." Skye had told us when
we were in Turton's, looking at the china and
glass, before Melia had gone and breathed too
heavily and upset things.

"Yeah. Well! I just thought I'd tell you," said
Jem.

I took a deep breath. "You and *Skye* are
going?"

"Yup." Jem nodded.

"On your own?"

She looked uncomfortable at that.

"Without me?"

Jem picked up a Smartie and lobbed it at her
mouth, and missed.

I said again, "Without *me*?"

"It's just... we didn't want you bringing Melia!"

"You mean, Skye didn't want me bringing
Melia."

"Not just Skye." Jem mumbled it, apologetically. "Me, as well."

"But you're her friend!" She was always going on about *my friend Jemma*. "She thinks you like her!"

"I do like her," said Jem. "I do. Honestly! She's really sweet and I hate it when people like Daisy make fun of her, but you've got to admit she does ruin things!"

I couldn't deny it. It really was quite impossible to relax and enjoy yourself when you had Melia with you. You had to be on your guard every single second, and even then she could take you by surprise and go plunging off into disaster.

"So I won't bring her," I said.

Jem looked at me, doubtfully. "Won't your mum make you?"

"She won't *make* me." She'd just be disappointed, that was all. I was a bit disappointed myself, to tell the truth. As a rule I really enjoy doing things for people, even if they don't always turn out quite right. I'd thought it would be fun, looking after Melia!

I was beginning to wonder if I would have to settle for a career change. Something *not* to do with people. An electrician, maybe, like Dad. Or a TV celebrity chef. Or a plumber. Except I couldn't really get very enthusiastic about sinks and pipes and stuff, and the last time I'd tried cooking anything it had all ended up in the bin and Angel had got food poisoning, or so she *said*. And on second thoughts I couldn't be an electrician cos of being what Dad calls a liability. I once plugged the wrong thing into the wrong socket and all the lights went out. I was only ten at the time, but Dad still says I should have known better. Probably, on the whole, I had to admit, I was not cut out for a career in electricity.

So what *was* I cut out for? If I couldn't even look after Melia! I heaved a sigh. Why did life have to be so complicated?

"I knew you'd be upset," said Jem.

"I'm not upset," I said. Though I was, of course. "Anyway, we've solved the problem... I just won't bring her!"

"So have you checked with your mum?" Skye wanted to know, as we finished school on Friday afternoon.

"Not yet," I said. "But I will! Be round my place, eleven o'clock. You'll see!"

Mum was really good about it. I managed to get her on her own in the front room, while she was waiting for one of her ladies.

"It's just this once," I pleaded. "Cos last time, Mum, it was so embarrassing! She won't stop touching at things. And she knocked down all these glasses, and this woman got really angry with us, and then we went into Boots and she started using make-up, and it wasn't even testers, so we had to pay for it. We thought they'd arrest us or something!"

"Oh, dear," said Mum. "What a sorry tale! Never mind, she's only here for another week."

"But tomorrow!" I said. "What about tomorrow?"

"Don't worry about tomorrow, she can stay home. I'm going to be a bit busy, but your dad's around, and Tom. They can help out."

I said, "*Tom?*"

"Well, your dad."

"He won't let her take Rags out on her own, will he?"

"Of course he won't!"

"And he'll make sure she doesn't open the front door and let him escape?"

"She's not going to open the front door."

I said rather darkly that you never knew

what Melia was going to do. "You have to watch her all the time!"

"We'll watch her," said Mum. "You go out with your friends and have fun."

I was so looking forward to it! It was like a great weight had been lifted off my shoulders. I was going into town with Skye and Jem and *no Melia.* Yay!

And then, next morning, it all fell to pieces. It was Dad's fault. He is such a soft touch! Sometimes you just have to harden your heart. *I* hadn't enjoyed telling Melia that she couldn't come with us. Her face had immediately gone all wobbly. Her lips had puckered and her cheeks started to quiver.

"Not go with you?"

"Not today," I said. "It's just the three of us today." And then I shouted, "Sorry!" and rushed downstairs to play with Rags until the others arrived.

A few minutes later, I heard Dad's voice: "Hello! What's up with you?"

I went into the hall and saw Dad, sitting at the top of the stairs with his arm round Melia. Melia's big moon face stared tragically down at me. It was swimming in tears.

"What's the matter?" said Dad. "Who's upset you?"

Melia wiped her nose on her sleeve and pointed accusingly at me.

"Frankie? What's she done?"

"She won't let me go shopping with her!"

"Won't let you go shopping?"

Melia shook her head, waving it tragically to and fro.

Dad said, "Why's that?"

Melia hiccuped. "Cos she's mean!"

"Very mean," said Dad. He gazed down at me, reproachfully. "Why can't you take her with you?"

I wasn't quite brave enough to say, "Because

we don't want her." I muttered that it wasn't convenient.

"Not convenient?"

Reluctantly I said, "She messes things up."

"Pardon me?" Dad cupped a hand to his ear. "Say again?"

"She messes things up!"

"Oh, come on," said Dad, "it can't be that bad. Suppose I were to give you..." He put his hand in his pocket and pulled out some notes. "Suppose I were to give you a fiver to buy yourselves a bag of chips, or whatever it is you eat, how would that be?"

"Dad," I said, "that's bribery!"

"Well, of course it is," said Dad. "Nothing wrong with a good honest bribe! Not if it makes someone happy. Stops them crying. Eh?" He gave Melia a hug. "How about it?"

I tried to stand firm, but the sight of Melia's face got too much for me, and in the end I gave way. I guess I am a bit of a soft touch too. Mum always says that Rags has me under his paw, meaning that he knows how to get round me. *And he always knows when he's won.* Melia knew when she'd won. Her tears dried up as if by magic. She came hurtling down the stairs towards me.

"Thank you, Frankie, thank you, Frankie! Thank you, thank you, thank you!"

"Well, now," said Dad. "Doesn't that make it all worthwhile?"

I didn't reckon Skye and Jem were going to think so. The door bell rang at that moment, and with deep foreboding I went to answer it. They stood there on the doorstep, their faces wreathed in happy smiles. And then they saw Melia beaming at them, and the smiles faded.

"I'm coming shopping!" cried Melia.

"I couldn't help it." I mouthed the words, desperately. "It was Dad!"

"I'll tell you what," said Dad, "I'll give you a lift. Won't be a jiffy, you wait there."

Skye was glaring at me like I was some kind of low, creeping thing that had come sliming out from under a stone.

"You promised!" said Jem.

"I know," I said, "I know. But look! Look what I've got!" I held out Dad's fiver. "We can share it!"

Skye gave me this look; really withering.

"*Traitor*," hissed Jem.

Dad arrived with the car and we all climbed in. Skye sat in the front, very stiff and straight. I sat at the back, sandwiched between Jem (scowling) and Melia (wriggling).

"You're all being very solemn," said Dad. "Taken a vow of silence, have you?"

Nobody said anything. Dad caught my eye in the mirror. "Cat got your tongue?"

For some reason, Melia found this funny. She

went off into one of her great gurgles of laughter, rocking backwards and forwards on the seat.

"Well, at least someone's happy," said Dad.

He dropped us off at the entrance to the shopping centre. "OK, girls, there you are. Spend wisely!"

"Where we going, where we going?" demanded Melia. She bounced energetically up and down. "Go back to Boots, do the make-up!"

"No," I said, "we've done the make-up. We're going to buy a present for Skye's nan."

"You just make sure you keep hold of her," said Skye.

"I will!" I said. And I did. I clamped my arm very tightly through hers so that we were practically glued together. It wasn't very comfortable, but at least she couldn't break away or make any sudden lunges. Skye and Jem walked ahead, like they were nothing to do with us, which didn't stop Melia shouting out after them.

"Hey, Jemma! Hey, Skye! We're going shopping!"

And then she'd do one of her clumsy twirls and kick me in the ankle or stamp on one of my feet, and Skye would turn round and hiss, like really exasperated, and Jem would pull a face, and I'd say, "Melia, be quiet!" but only half-heartedly cos I mean she wasn't doing anything wrong. She was just enjoying herself.

We went up the escalator to China and Glass and Skye gave me this look which said, as plain as anything, *just watch it!* I clamped Melia even tighter, pinning her to me with superhuman force, but still she almost managed to cause disaster.

"Frankie, look!" she cried. "There's a mug like your mum's one that you broke!" Her free arm went flailing out. I jerked her away just in time.

"Don't *do* that!"

Skye rolled her eyes heavenwards. Jem said, "You broke your mum's mug? The one I helped you choose?"

She hadn't helped me *choose*, but she had been with me. I'd told her about pansies being one of Mum's favourite flowers.

"How'd you break it?" said Jem.

"I didn't." I jabbed a finger at Melia. "She did."

"Oh." Jem nodded.

"Frankie!" Melia clutched me, excitedly. "You could buy another one!"

"I can't," I said. "I don't have enough money."

I had Dad's fiver, but that was for sharing with Jem and Skye, to make up for me bringing Melia and ruining their shopping experience. In any case, a fiver wasn't enough. Mum's mug had been a superior mug. Bone china! I'd had to use nearly two weeks' pocket money.

"For goodness' sake," said Skye. "Let's go and get Nan's present before we're thrown out."

"Yes, and then we can decide what we want to spend Dad's money on."

I kept Melia clamped so tight while Skye was buying her present that she didn't have a chance to get at anything. She'd even stopped shouting out, so I couldn't really see that Skye had any reason to complain. I felt quite jubilant as we made our way back to the escalator. We'd been all round China and Glass and Melia hadn't touched anything, she hadn't broken anything, she hadn't even breathed on anything. She was really behaving quite nicely. Maybe I wouldn't need a career change, after all!

"Let's go to the Pick 'n' Mix and spend Dad's money," I said.

"Yesss!" Jem liked that. "Let's buy all the really sticky icky yucky stuff we can find!"

All the stuff our mums wouldn't approve of.

"*Pink* stuff."

"Green stuff!"

"Yellow stuff!"

"JUNK FOOD!"

We chorused it, exultantly; even Skye. She seemed a bit more relaxed now that she'd managed to get her nan's present and we hadn't been thrown out.

"Can I have junk food?" said Melia.

I said, "You can have whatever you want."

"Sticky Fingaz?" Melia clapped her hands, excitedly. "Jem, I'm going to have Sticky Fingaz!"

"You bet," said Jem.

But she never had them. On our way to the Pick 'n' Mix she suddenly announced, in ringing tones, that she had to go. I said, "Go where?"

"*Go*," shouted Melia. "Frankie, I've got to go!" And she did a little clumping jig and clutched urgently at herself with both hands. God, it even embarrassed me! I didn't dare look at Skye. I gave Melia a bit of a shove and pointed her in the direction of the Ladies.

"Over there! We'll wait for you."

I just hoped she went through the door marked LADIES and not the one marked GENTLEMEN. They didn't have the little ladies and gentlemen figures, and I wasn't sure how good Melia was at reading.

"Should have gone with her," said Skye.

Rather crossly, because I knew she was right, I snapped, "I can't go everywhere with her! She's got to learn."

We all watched, anxiously, as Melia loped off, still clutching at herself. I breathed a sigh of relief as she disappeared through the right door.

"I'm really sorry about bringing her," I said. "It was Dad!"

"Yes, you said," said Jem.

Skye just grunted, like, "Hmph!"

We sat on one of the low walls surrounding a flower bed and settled down to wait for Melia.

"You must admit," I said, "it's all worked out. You've got your nan's prezzie and now we can go and spend Dad's fiver."

"Maybe," said Skye.

What did she mean, maybe? "We're going to! Soon as Melia comes back."

"*If* she comes back. What's she up to? She's been in there for ages."

"Should have gone with her," said Jem.

"I told you," I said. "She's got to learn."

"I bet she's locked herself in and doesn't know how to get out."

"She might already have come out," said Skye.

I frowned. "How could she come out without us noticing?" We'd been watching the whole time. Well, most of the time.

"You know what she's like... could be half way up the High Street by now."

"You'd better go and look," said Skye. "Me and Jem'll go on."

I heaved myself up and went stomping off towards the Ladies. I couldn't believe that Melia had come out and we hadn't seen her, but it was true she had been in there for a long time. I stuck my head round the door. The place was empty! Butterflies began swarming in my stomach.

"Melia," I yelled, "are you there?"

Slowly, one of the cubicle doors opened. In a small voice, Melia said, "Frankie?"

I rushed over. "What are you doing?"

A stifled giggle burst out of her. It sounded uncertain, like she was scared I was going to be cross. "My trousers are broken!"

"*What?*"

"My trousers are broken!"

She shuffled out, holding the trousers up with one hand.

I said, "What d'you mean, they're broken?"

"They won't do up!"

She'd gone and busted the zip. She must really have yanked at it, cos it wasn't just stuck, it was hanging right off.

"There's got to be a button," I said. But there wasn't. There wasn't any sort of fastening at all. *Now* what were we supposed to do?

"Just keep a hold of them," I said. "Whatever you do, don't let go!"

She sulked the whole way home, whining, because she'd missed out on her Sticky Fingaz, while I thought glumly, all over again, about being a plumber.

We caught up with Jem and Skye at the bus stop.

"What's happened now?" Skye said. "Why is she clutching herself?"

Melia said, "My trousers have broken and Frankie won't let me go to Pick 'n' Mix!"

CHAPTER EIGHT

There was no sign of either Jem or Skye on Monday morning. I waited as long as I could, but in the end I had to give up and go on by myself with Melia. Rather irritably I told her to "Stop hopping! Why do you have to keep doing it all the time? It's totally stupid!"

I was aware even as I said it that I was being mean. How did Melia know why she did things? She just did them. She just wanted to be happy.

When I snapped at her, her face fell. She said, "Sorry, Frankie, sorry, Frankie, s—"

"It's all right," I said. "But just walk normally, can't you?"

She tried; she really did. I could see her lips bunched up and her fingers all stiff and splayed with the effort of concentrating. She still didn't walk normally. It was something to do with her arms and legs not matching up; one of them always seemed to be moving at the wrong time in the wrong direction. Maybe that was why she hopped. Maybe she found it easier.

She shot me this worried glance, like Rags when he's not sure he's doing the right thing.

"It's OK," I said. "You can hop, if you want."

Gratefully, she did a little skip. "Where's Jem 'n' Skye?"

"Dunno," I said. "Obviously late."

Except that Skye was never late. I guessed she must have gone on ahead, not wanting to be seen with me and Melia. Jem would be late because Jem often was.

"I like Jem," said Melia. "She's my friend! Skye gets cross with me."

"Oh, that's just Skye," I said. "You don't want to take any notice of her."

We reached Melia's school and I watched her lollop eagerly across the playground. Two girls ran to meet her, crying, "Melia, Melia!" I was glad she was popular. She didn't deserve to be picked on all the time, just because she was a bit clumsy and awkward and breathed too heavily. She saw me watching and waved.

"Bye, Frankie!"

I waved back. "Bye, Melia!"

I suddenly found that I was feeling incredibly protective. This was what it was all about! *Caring* for people. Watching out for them. I was back on track! I didn't need to be a plumber, after all. I was a *people* person.

I raced back up the road and swung in through the school gates quite jauntily. If Skye didn't want to walk with us any more, that was her problem. I reckon it is truly sad to care so much about the impression you are making, and what people might think. I was just glad that *one* of my friends wasn't like that. Me and Jem could get on perfectly well without Skye and her snooty ways.

And then I reached our classroom, squeezing in just seconds before the bell, and there was Skye, sitting at her desk, and there was Jem, sitting next to her. She was leaning back, talking to Rhianna Shah, and had all her books spread out ready for history. She couldn't just have got there. She'd been there for ages! I banged my bag down, next to her.

"What happened?" I hissed. "I waited for you!"

She was saved from having to reply by the arrival of Mrs Datchett, who has ears like a bat and goes totally ballistic if anyone dares to so much as whisper. It wasn't till break time that they told me.

"We're really sorry—"

"Really *really*."

"But we just can't take Melia any more!"

They'd been talking about it behind my back. Arranging to meet up without me. They were obviously feeling guilty; even Skye. Pleadingly she said, "If it was just once or twice, it wouldn't be so bad, but it's *all the time*."

"We know it's not her fault," said Jem.

"We know she can't help it."

"It's just the way she is."

"You mean, you're embarrassed to be seen with her," I said.

"No! Well – y-yes. Maybe. Just a bit. I mean, Saturday..." Jem's voice trailed off.

"You promised you wouldn't bring her," said Skye.

"I told you! It was Dad."

"Yes. Well. Anyway." Skye pulled a face. "We're really sorry."

"We are," said Jem. "Honest!"

"So what am I going to tell Melia? When she wants to know where you are?"

They fell silent at that.

"What am I s'pposed to say?"

"Could just say we're busy," mumbled Jem.

"What, like every single day?"

Jem stuck a finger in her mouth and nibbled at a nail. Skye stared down fixedly at her feet.

I said, "*Well?*"

"Well..."

Skye shuffled, uneasily. Jem tore off a chunk of nail.

"Oh, don't worry," I said. "I'll just tell her the truth... they don't want to be seen with you any more. They're ashamed! Cos you do stupid things all the time and it embarrasses them.

It's OK, she won't mind, she has learning difficulties. Won't matter to her. She doesn't have feelings same as the rest of us."

Jem removed her finger from her mouth and squeaked in protest. Skye, in shocked tones, said, "*Frankie!*"

"We don't want her to be hurt," whispered Jem.

"Oh, I expect she's used to it by now," I said. "It probably happens all the time."

With that I went marching off across the yard. I spent the rest of break on my own, simmering in a corner. Daisy Hooper saw me and said, "What's up with you?" to which I smartly replied, "Mind your own business," so then of course she immediately knew that we'd had a falling out and went round telling everyone.

At lunch time the others tried to make it up. They came and sat next to me, like nothing had ever happened. Skye said, "This is so ridiculous! Just because we don't want you bringing Melia with you wherever we go."

"I have to take her in to school," I said. "I can't do anything about that."

"That's OK," said Skye. "You can tell her we're having to go in early."

"Yes, you don't have to tell her we don't like her," said Jem. "That would be unkind. And anyway," she added, "it's not true. We do like her!"

"You just don't want to be seen with her."

They shoved the food round their plates and didn't say anything.

"What about in the afternoon?" I said. "I s'ppose you're staying late, then."

Jem brightened. "Yes, we could be staying for music lessons, or – or detentions, or – or choir practice, or—"

I felt like picking up my plate and dumping

it on her. Jem obviously realised she'd said the wrong thing.

"Well, anyway," she muttered.

"Look, we don't mind *occasionally*," said Skye. "Just not all the time. I don't think that's being unreasonable. Do you?" She nudged at Jem, who immediately swallowed and choked on her food.

"You mean, like, maybe once a week?" I said.

"Yes!" Skye nodded. "Or even twice. Just not every day." She smiled, encouragingly. "Is that OK?"

I speared a Brussels sprout and sat for a moment, looking at it. I *loathe* Brussels sprouts. "I don't really want to talk about it any more," I said.

"Probably wisest," agreed Skye.

"Yes, cos whatever happens –" Jem said it earnestly – "we don't want to quarrel! We haven't quarrelled, have we?"

"Absolutely not!" said Skye. "Well, I haven't."

I hadn't, either. I don't believe in quarrelling, it makes you all cross and bothered, and somebody has to say sorry before you can make things up, and if you're the one that says it you get to feel resentful, cos why should it be you and not one of the others, 'specially if you weren't the one that was in the wrong? Which in this case *I wasn't.* It wasn't my fault I'd had to take Melia with me.

"We are still friends," said Jem, "aren't we?"

"I s'ppose so," I said.

We'd patched things up, but it wasn't the same. For the rest of the day they went out of their way to be extra 'specially nice to me. It felt very odd. Skye asked if I needed any help with my maths homework. Jem insisted on giving me half a KitKat. In English, which was the last period of the day, Skye even passed me a note saying *I really DO have a music lesson at 3.30*. Skye never passes notes! It just wasn't normal.

When school let out I went off by myself to collect Melia. Skye had her music lesson – "Frankie, I'm going to my music lesson now!" Jem didn't have anything. She walked with me as far as the gate, then stopped.

"Oh, look," she said, "I don't mind coming with you, if you like."

"Please don't bother," I said.

I was feeling a bit hurt, to tell the truth. You expect your friends to be there for you no matter what. Jem started to bleat a protest, but I cut her short.

"'s all right," I said. "Me and Melia can manage by ourselves."

The minute I'd said it, I wished I hadn't. If I'd accepted her offer we could have made up properly and then it would have been me and

Jem together and Skye the odd one out. Now it was me.

Melia wanted to know why I hadn't brought the others with me.

"Where are they?"

I said, "Skye's got a music lesson."

"Where's Jem?"

"Jem's... in detention," I said. And serve her right! It was where she ought to be.

We arrived home to find Mum in something of a froth over the state of our bedroom. *Angel's* bedroom, as Mum reminded us.

"Poor Angel keeps her things so neat and tidy! She'd have a fit if she saw what you two had done to it. Are you aware of the dreadful mess you've made?"

I had to admit that I wasn't. I find that when you are living in it, mess doesn't seem like mess, it just seems like the natural state of things. Quite cosy and comfortable.

"Well, I advise you," said Mum, "to go and have a look... pretend you're someone going in there for the first time."

"I'll pretend I'm you," I said.

"You do that," said Mum.

So I did, and I saw what she meant.

"Look at this!" I said to Melia. "Could it *be* more disgusting? Clothes all over the place!" I kicked a pair of jeans out of the way. They flew up and draped themselves over the dressing table. Angel's frilly pink dressing table with the triple mirrors that she could admire herself in. Melia giggled.

"It's not funny," I said, still being Mum. "It's very squalid and repulsive and you and me are going to clear it up. Just don't touch any of Angel's things. OK?"

"OK!" Melia nodded.

"First we'll pick up the clothes," I said, "then we'll get rid of all the plates and cups and stuff, and all the books and shoes and – everything!"

Once I get going on a job, I like to do it thoroughly. It's the getting going that's difficult; I quite enjoy it once I've started. As soon as we'd cleared some floor space, and put the clothes away, and taken all the dirty dishes down to the kitchen, I said that we would dust and vacuum.

"Make it, like, really spotless! I'll vacuum, and you can dust."

I like using the vacuum; I like the way it goes splurging round, sucking things up. It is very satisfying. I am not so keen on dusting as I find it is a rather fiddly sort of job, especially when there's loads of stuff that needs picking up and putting back. I told Melia not to bother.

"When there's stuff that needs moving, just blow. And *don't touch anything on the shelves.*"

Angel's shelves are crammed full of little itty

bitty things that she likes to collect. Breakable things, mostly. I might have known that Melia couldn't resist.

"What's happening?" I shrieked, as something whizzed past my ear and landed in front of the vacuum cleaner. "What are you doing?"

She'd gone and knocked a glass animal to the floor. I only just managed to avoid sucking it up with the vacuum cleaner. Fortunately it wasn't broken, but something inside me just suddenly snapped.

I said, "Listen, *doofus.*" Melia stood there, blinking. I jabbed at her. "I thought I told you not to touch?"

It was like the top of my head was about to explode. I felt like smashing things and shrieking. Instead, I jabbed at Melia again; quite hard.

"Didn't I tell you? Didn't I say..." I jabbed again, and she stumbled and fell backwards against one of the beds. *"Don't touch any of Angel's stuff?"*

Melia cringed away from me. "Frankie, I didn't," she whimpered. "I didn't!"

"So how did it get on the floor? If you didn't knock it there?"

"I just blew on it, like you said."

"I didn't say blow a gale!"

It was like Turton's, all over again. Breathing on the glasses. Getting us into trouble. I wasn't surprised Skye and Jem didn't want to be seen with us any more.

I stuck the glass animal back on the shelf. "You're lucky it's not broken," I said, "cos this time I'd have told on you. I don't see why I should always get the blame for everything. Like when you messed up Tom's science project. *Oh, it's Frankie! It's always Frankie.* You never owned up! *And* you broke Mum's mug!"

Melia stuffed her fist into her mouth and

chewed agitatedly at her knuckles, staring up at me as she did so. Her eyes were big and frightened. I began to feel a bit ashamed.

"It was just that it was Mum's favourite," I said. "I got it for her birthday. It took me ages to save up for it. Oh, look, stop eating yourself!" I had these visions of her gnawing her knuckles down to the bone and it would all be my fault for yelling at her. "Let's just get on and finish the room. You can vacuum, if you like."

She brightened up at that; it's what she'd wanted all along. While I went round blowing – *gently* – Melia went round, bashing and battering, with the vacuum cleaner, cheerfully sucking up everything in her path, including a stray sock that had got overlooked. After which, the vacuum cleaner didn't work any more.

Determinedly, I didn't say a word. I simply unplugged the thing and took it downstairs to the kitchen, with Melia trailing apprehensively behind me. I had this idea I might be able to do something with a screwdriver, like Dad had once done when I'd accidentally vacuumed up one of Rags' squeaky toys. It was just bad luck that Mum and Angel came in while I was still working on it. I'd have got it going again, I know I would!

"Oh, God," cried Angel, "now she's gone and broken the vacuum cleaner!"

"Frankie, what have you done?" said Mum.

"It's all right," I panted, wrestling with the screwdriver, "it's just a sock."

"Well, don't yank at it like that!"

"She's broken it," said Angel. "She breaks everything!"

Mum sighed, and shook her head.

"We were cleaning the room," I said, "like you wanted."

Angel narrowed her eyes. "I hope you haven't been touching any of my stuff?"

I said, "I haven't been anywhere near your rotten stuff."

"You better not have!"

I became aware of Melia's hand creeping into mine. I squeezed it, reassuringly.

"I'm going up to have a look," said Angel. "If I find you've touched anything—"

"Well, you won't," I said, "cos we haven't. Wouldn't want to! It's all rubbish."

That night, as we lay in bed, I whispered to Melia that I was sorry I'd poked her and called her doofus.

"I know you were only trying to help."

It is what I do myself. All the time! I just try to help. Things simply have this annoying habit of going wrong.

A sudden gurgle came from Melia's bed.

"What?" I said.

"Doofus!"

I heard the mattress creak as she threw

herself about, giggling. A few little prickles of anxiety ran down my spine. Doofus was a word I'd picked up from Dad. I'd heard him use it on the telephone one day, when he was ringing the Council to complain about something. He'd said, "*Listen, doofus!*" I'd remembered it, cos it was funny. But I didn't think, probably, that it was very complimentary.

"Hey, Melia," I said.

She was still giggling.

"Oi!" I leant across and prodded her. "You'd better not tell Mum I called you that," I said. "I don't think she'd like it."

CHAPTER NINE

Next morning, at breakfast, Mum was going on about the vacuum cleaner.

"Your dad got it working again, but it still beats me how you managed to get a sock stuck in there."

"Guess I just didn't notice it," I said.

"Who could miss something the size of a sock?"

"She could," said Angel; while at exactly the

same moment Melia spluttered, "Doofus!" and spat a mouthful of cereal across the table. Tom went, "Bloody hell!" I found one of Melia's feet and trod on it.

"*What* did she say?" said Angel.

"Didn't say anything," I said.

"She did! She distinctly said something."

"Well, whatever it was, she wasn't saying it to you."

"Excuse *me*," said Angel, "I wasn't aware people were conducting private conversations. How rude is that? In front of everybody."

"She was saying it," I said, "to *herself.*"

Melia put a finger to her lips. "Not supposed to mention."

"Mention what?"

"Doo-fus." She mouthed the word, silently, then giggled and shot me this sly glance, like we were in some kind of conspiracy together.

"Say again?" said Angel.

There are times when you have to move fast. I did so.

"OK!" I shoved back my chair and grabbed Rags' lead from its hook on the door. "Let's go!"

Melia giggled all the way up the road. She also hopped on and off the kerb. "Doofus!" she chanted. "Doooo-fus! Doooo—"

"Stop it," I said. "If you don't stop it, I'll tell Mum it was you that vacuumed the sock!"

Later that day I got Dad by himself for a few minutes.

"Dad, what's a doofus?" I said.

"A dimwit," said Dad.

"You mean, like, someone stupid?" I thought about it for a second. "Was that person at the Council stupid?"

"Which person at the Council?"

"The one you shouted at! You called them doofus."

Dad looked a bit ashamed. "I was under extreme provocation."

I reckoned I was under extreme provocation too, what with my supposedly best friends deserting me, and Melia nearly breaking one of Angel's glass animals, not to mention sucking socks into the vacuum cleaner. Plus she'd broken Mum's mug. *And* messed with Tom's science project. *And* I always seemed to have to take the blame. But I knew Mum would say that was no excuse for calling her doofus. Not if it meant stupid.

"It's not really something you should call people," said Dad.

I said, "Not even in fun?"

"Well... yes, that would probably be OK. So long as you were just joking."

But I hadn't been joking, I'd been furiously angry. I made a solemn vow, right there and then, that for the rest of Melia's time with us

I would be kind and patient and understanding. No matter what she did, I would not let myself be provoked.

There was no sign of Skye or Jem at our usual place on Monday morning, but that was all right; I wasn't expecting them to be there. Melia was doing her hopping thing again, bashing into people and not looking where she was going; but that was all right too. That was just Melia. You only had to think of people being blown up, or people dying of starvation, to realise that Melia hopping wasn't really all that important. So I didn't yell at her, I just very firmly took her by the hand and clamped her to my side. So what if Daisy Hooper came along and jeered? As it happened, she didn't; but even if she had I wouldn't have let it bother me. In the general scheme of things, what was Daisy Hooper? Lower than an earth worm, cos earth worms are *useful*.

I think what I was being was philosophical. I think that's the word. It's what Dad says when things don't go according to plan: you have to be philosophical. Meaning, I guess, make the best of things.

I was trying very hard to make the best of things. I did find it difficult, though, at school.

Skye and Jem were going out of their way to pretend that nothing was wrong. They were being just *sooo* polite and *sooo* considerate. I knew it was because they were feeling guilty. They were trying to make up to me for the way they had behaved, but I had this little knot inside me which just kept getting tighter and tighter.

By the end of the week I was feeling really miserable. I didn't have much patience when Melia started nagging me, Saturday morning, to take her to the shopping centre.

"*Pleeeze*, Frankie! *Pleeeze!* Let's go shopping, Frankie!"

I wasn't in the mood for shopping. I pointed out that we had gone to the shopping centre last Saturday *and* the Saturday before.

"I don't spend my entire life going shopping. There are other things to do."

Even if I wasn't quite sure what. We'd already taken Rags for his walk. Angel was off with her latest boyfriend, Tom was in his room, Mum was with one of her ladies, Dad was out working. It was just me and Melia. I hadn't made any plans with Skye or Jem, and while we don't always do things together at weekends it was hard to escape the horrid nagging suspicion that they might have made plans without me. I didn't *think* that they would; but they just might have.

"Frankie, Frankie, please!" Melia was dabbing at me, patting me with her hands. "Please, Frankie!"

"There wouldn't be any point," I said. "I haven't got any money."

"Got your pocket money," said Melia.

I said, "I'm saving that."

"Got the money your dad gave you." She shot me this sly glance. She could be quite cunning, at times; I thought she'd have forgotten about Dad's money. "We could go to the Pick 'n' Mix, Frankie! Cos we didn't go there last week, did we?"

"No, we didn't," I said. We'd been too busy hustling Melia back home before her trousers fell down.

"So we could go there today?"

"I'm not spending Dad's money on sweets," I said. "That's going towards a new mug for Mum. *To replace the one you broke.*"

For a moment she looked uncertain, but then she brightened. "I've got pocket money! I could buy sweets."

In the end, I gave in. I knew she wouldn't let up cos once she got going on something she never stopped. Besides, what else did I have to do? Nothing. Just sit around the house and brood as I pictured Skye and Jem giggling together without me. My two best friends, planning things behind my back! If they could still be called best friends. Best friends don't desert you when you need them most. Cos honestly, it wasn't much fun on my own with Melia.

We went to the Pick 'n' Mix and she bought some Sticky Fingaz for herself and a big Munchy bar for me. I didn't really want a Munchy bar but Melia seemed anxious for me to have one and I thought it would be ungracious to refuse. While we were perched on the edge of the Wishing Pool, with me half-heartedly nibbling and Melia sucking on her Sticky Fingaz, I saw this girl from our class coming towards us. Melissa Diaz. I didn't honestly expect her to do more than just say hello, cos she's one of Daisy

Hooper's gang, at least I always thought she was. I was quite surprised when she stopped and settled down to chat.

"Where are the others?" she said.

She meant Skye and Jem. People were used to seeing us together.

"We're not stuck with super glue," I said. "We do go places on our own occasionally."

"Someone told me you'd quarrelled."

Scornfully, I said, "We don't do quarrels."

"Oh. OK!" Mel shrugged. "Must have got it wrong."

"Who was it, anyway?" I said. "I s'ppose it was Daisy."

"She makes things up," said Mel. "I don't hang out with her any more."

"Really?" I said. "Since when?"

"Since for practically ever... not since the beginning of term, if you want to know."

I said, "Why? What did she do?"

"Didn't do anything, particularly. I just went off her."

"Well, she's not a very nice person," I said.

Mel rolled her eyes. "Tell me about it! D'you remember, at juniors, that mousy girl? Elsa?"

"She ran away."

"Yes, and that was cos of Daisy. *Bullying* her."

I said, "I never knew that."

Mel said darkly there were lots of things about Daisy that I didn't know.

"She can be so mean you wouldn't believe! I thought that was really nasty the other day, when she was making fun of that girl."

"Which girl?"

"That one she'd seen you with? The one you said had learning difficulties?"

"Oh, you mean M—" I stopped. Omigod! Where *was* Melia? She'd gone! One minute she'd been perched on the edge of the Wishing Pool, happily slurping her Sticky

Fingaz; the next minute, not a trace.

"What's the matter?" said Mel.

I said, "Melia! She was here, just a second ago. Right here, next to me! Didn't you see her? You must have seen her!"

Mel shook her head, doubtfully. "I don't think so."

"But she was right here!"

"I didn't really notice. Maybe she's just..."

"What?"

"Gone to buy something?"

I was about to say she didn't have any money, but that wasn't quite true, she did still have some of her pocket money.

"The Pick 'n' Mix." I said. "She could have gone back to the Pick 'n' Mix!"

I set off at a mad gallop. Mel galloped with me. I was so sure Melia would be there; there just didn't seem any other place she would go. But while everybody remembered her, it seemed that nobody had seen her. Not since we'd been there half an hour ago, buying Sticky Fingaz.

"I just don't know where she could be!" I wailed.

"Could she have gone home?" said Mel.

"No!" I shook my head. "She wouldn't know how to get there."

"So maybe she's just, like... wandering around? Looking at things? I mean... she wouldn't go with anyone, would she?"

That was my big fear. I knew she'd been warned not to talk to strangers, cos she'd told me so herself – "Mustn't talk to strangers!" But suppose someone offered to buy her some sweets? She might be tempted to go with them. I began to feel a bit sick and shaky.

"Think," urged Mel. "Where else does she know? Apart from the sweet shop?"

"Um... mm... Boots!" It suddenly came to me. "She knows Boots!"

I would have given anything to find Melia breaking open lipsticks and smearing them over herself; but we went round the whole store and there wasn't a sign of her. I was beginning to panic. Mel turned on me, quite fiercely.

"Where else? There's got to be somewhere else! She must know other places."

I forced myself to calm down. I thought back to that first Saturday, when she'd embarrassed us in the HMV shop, shouting out the names of bands at the top of her voice.

"HMV," I said.

We raced there at breakneck speed. I prayed that I would hear Melia's loud, tuneless voice; but again, there was no sign of her.

"O-kay." Mel said it very slowly and carefully. "What about... " She gazed round. "The Ladies! What about the Ladies?"

"Yessss!"

She knew the Ladies, all right. That was where she would be!

But she wasn't. And by now even Mel was starting to wonder if we should go to the police.

"But how do we find them?" I whimpered. "I don't know where the police station is!"

"You have to ring 999," said Mel. "Or maybe we could go into Turton's and get them to do a thing on their loudspeaker system like when they've found a child? *Would the mother of whoever it is please—*"

"Turton's!" I practically screamed it. "She could be in Turton's!"

And oh, she was! We arrived, puffing and blowing, just as she was ambling out into the precinct.

"MELIA!" I charged up to her. She beamed at me, like totally unconcerned. "Where have you been?"

"Been in the shop."

"Why? What for?"

Her eyes slid away. "Just wanted to."

"I've been worried sick," I said. "You know you're not supposed to go wandering off like that!"

She chewed at her bottom lip, but she didn't seem very repentant. More like she was trying to stifle a giggle.

"We've been looking all over for you," said Mel. "We were going to call the p'lice!"

That sobered her. She clutched at the front of her anorak and looked at me, big-eyed.

"I still might," I said. "Get them to lock you up! *Honestly*." I hooked my arm very firmly through hers, gluing her to my side. "You gave me the most horrible fright I've ever had! What d'you think your mum'd say if she came out of hospital and I had to tell her I'd gone and lost you?"

She chewed again at her lip, but she wasn't

giggling any more. She muttered, "Sorry, Frankie."

"I should think you jolly well ought to be! I'm going to take you home, now. I've had enough of this place."

"I'll be off, then," said Mel. "Glad it all ended happily."

I called after her, "Thanks for staying with me!"

She flapped a hand. "Don't mention it."

I genuinely did feel grateful to her; it is horrid being on your own in that sort of situation. I'd been really scared for a few minutes. Melia wanted to know if Mel was my friend. I told her she was just a girl in my class.

"Not like Jem 'n' Skye?"

I said no, not like Jem and Skye. Jem and Skye had deserted me.

"Where *is* Jem?" said Melia.

"Dunno," I said. "At home, I s'ppose."

"Why didn't she come shopping with us?"

"Guess she didn't want to."

"Why not?"

"I dunno. Probably had other things to do."

"Did Skye have other things to do?"

"Probably."

"What sort of th—"

"I don't know! I don't know what they're doing. And why are you clutching at your coat like that? You haven't gone and busted another zip, have you?"

She said she hadn't, but she still went on clutching. I told her not to. "It looks really stupid!"

"Doofus!" cried Melia; and she giggled, and clutched even tighter. I gave up at that. I just wanted to get her safely indoors.

We arrived home to find that Mum was still in the front room, seeing to one of her ladies; Tom, presumably, was still in his room, Angel and Dad were still out. We went through to the kitchen, where Rags was asleep in his basket. As soon as he saw us he came bounding over, full of his usual joy. Melia, still clutching at herself, screamed, "Down, Rags, careful, you'll break it!"

"Break what?" I said.

Beaming, she unzipped her anorak. "Got a present for you."

Omigod! It was Mum's mug...

CHAPTER TEN

"Melia, where did you get that from?" I said.

She held it out. "It's for you... for your mum."

"But where did you get it?"

Her eyes slid away. "Bought it with my pocket money!"

But I knew that she hadn't. For one thing, she'd already spent half her pocket money on sweets. For another, the mug wasn't in a box. It wasn't even in a bag.

"It's for you," she said.

I swallowed. "What happened to the box?"

"Wasn't in a box."

"What about the bag?"

"Threw it away."

I said, "Why? What d'you do that for?"

"Didn't want it." She pushed the mug at me. "For your mum."

I didn't want it. It was stolen property!

"Same like the one you broke," said Melia.

I opened my mouth, automatically, to say "*I didn't break it!*" But at that moment my mobile started up. I snatched at it, gratefully. It was Jem, calling to ask how I was. Like I'd been off sick, or something. *Guilt*, I thought. But I was pleased, all the same.

"Hang on," I said. "I'll just move to another room."

One of the problems of sharing with Melia, it was really difficult to be private. The only

place in the house where you could be sure
she wouldn't follow was the toilet. She'd probably
have crammed in there if I'd let her. Even as it
was, she trailed along the landing with me.

"Melia, d'you mind?" I said.

Jem giggled. "What's going on?"

I said, "Nothing. It's just Melia."

"You sound, like, sort of frazzled."

"We've been into town," I said.

"Not round the shops? Not with Melia?"

"She kept on at me. It just seemed easier, in
the end, to give in."

"Poor you," said Jem. "Was it awful?"

"What do you think?"

"I think you're a very good person," said
Jem.

Huh!

"Someone has to look after her," I said. "I
promised Mum, and once you've promised you
have to keep your word."

"So what happened?"

I banged down the toilet seat and sat on it. "She disappeared."

"How?"

"I don't know, she just did. I couldn't find her anywhere, I went into every shop we've ever been in, it was like a nightmare. I had these visions she'd gone off with someone. If Mel hadn't been with me, I don't know what I'd have done. It was really scary! We were going to dial 999, then Mel said maybe we could get Turton's to do one of their loudspeaker thingies? So we rushed off to Turton's and that's when we found her, and you'll never guess what?"

"What?"

"She's gone and stolen a mug!"

Jem said, "Stolen a mug?"

"Yes! Like the one she broke."

"*Melia?*" said Jem. "Stole a *mug*?"

How many times did you have to tell her something?

"You mean, she got away with it? Nobody caught her? Wow!"

Crossly I said, "It puts me in a very difficult situation."

"Why?"

"I can't give Mum a stolen mug!"

"Don't see why not," said Jem. "Who's to know?"

"*I'd* know!"

"Yes, but you didn't steal it. Is that what she went off to do? Get a mug? It's quite sweet, when you stop to think about it."

"Doesn't seem very sweet to me," I said. "I was going out of my mind! If Mel hadn't been there—"

"Mel Diaz?"

Did we know any other Mels?

"What were you doing with her?"

"We met up," I said.

"You and Mel?"

I do so hate it when you have to keep repeating yourself.

"Moments like that," I said, "you're just so grateful someone's there for you."

There was a bit of a pause.

"I s'ppose you would be," said Jem.

We didn't speak much after that cos Melia started scraping at the door, wanting to know if I was still in there. She just hated it when she was shut out.

"Guess I'd better go," I said.

Jem said, "Yes, go and give your mum her mug."

I thought about it; I was tempted. I'm not a goody goody! I am always being told off for talking when I shouldn't, or passing notes in class, and once or twice I've even cheated on my homework. Well, I've copied from Skye, which I suppose is a form of cheating. But I just didn't feel I could give Mum a present that was stolen goods. I mean, imagine if the police came round. Mum could be put in prison!

On the other hand, if I told her about it I would have to confess to not having kept a proper eye on Melia. I knew I'd been irresponsible, gossiping away with Mel, eagerly listening to her dish the dirt on Daisy Hooper. I didn't want Mum thinking I'd let her down.

But then, in the end, my conscience got the better of me. Or maybe I was just scared, cos I mean, you never know. Someone might have been watching. They might even have followed us. They could be waiting, even now, to see whether we would go back to Turton's and own up.

I waited till I could get Mum on her own, then let it all come tumbling out.

"I know I should have watched her more

carefully, but honestly, Mum, I only took my eye off her for about two seconds! She was just sitting there, eating her sweets. Next thing I knew, she'd gone."

"Well, don't beat yourself up about it," said Mum. "All's well that ends well. She didn't come to any harm."

"No, but then when we got back home she gave me this." I held out the mug. "Mum, I think she stole it!"

Unlike Angel, who lives in a perpetual rage from the minute she gets up to the minute she goes to bed, Mum almost never loses her cool. Dad has been known to, just occasionally, like when he called the Council and shouted "Doofus!" down the telephone. I had shouted doofus at Melia, so that made me just as bad. Mum would never, ever do anything like that. Even now, when I was offering her stolen property, she didn't blink.

"Are you sure about this?" she said. "You're telling me she just picked it up and walked out with it?"

"She must have done! There isn't any box – there isn't any bag. And she'd already spent most of her pocket money."

"What would make her steal a mug?" wondered Mum.

"Cos it was her that broke your one. She won't admit it, she pretends it was me, but she knows, really, that it was her. Like it was her," I said bitterly, "that got the sock stuck in the vacuum cleaner."

"And you took the blame!"

"Only cos she gets frightened. Anyway," I said, "I'm used to it. I'm always getting the blame."

"It was Melia who upset Tom's science project, wasn't it?" said Mum. "And you took the blame for that too." She suddenly hugged me. "Poor old you! It's been a tough time, hasn't it? But you've done so well! I'm really proud of you. Your dad never thought you'd stay the course. Bitten off more than you can chew, that's what he thought. But you've proved him wrong! We could never have taken Melia if it hadn't been for you."

I could feel my cheeks glowing, bright pink. I am not used to being praised!

"Don't worry," said Mum. "Only another few days, then we'll be back to normal. Do you reckon you can last that long?"

I assured her that I could. I am not someone that gives up.

"I'm afraid Melia is even more demanding than I thought," said Mum.

I suddenly realised something. "Mum, you're calling her Melia!" I said.

"Yes." Mum laughed. "I obviously caught it from you! Now, I wonder what we do about this mug? I could either put it in the cupboard and forget how we came by it, or I could take it back to Turton's first thing Monday morning and pay for it. Which do you think?"

"Couldn't we just give it back to them?" I said. "Why do we have to pay?"

"I suppose we could just give it back – but it was my favourite mug! I'd really like to keep it."

"But I wanted to buy it for you," I said. "I don't want you to have to buy it for yourself." And then I remembered: "I could give you £5 towards it!"

"Oh, Frankie, I can't take your money," said Mum.

"No," I said, "I want you to. Anyway, it was Dad's money, really. He gave it to me last week, for letting Melia come shopping with us. He *bribed* me. Only then Melia's trousers went and fell down and we had to come home, so I've still got the money. Please, Mum, say you'll take it!"

"Well, if it's going to make you happy," said Mum.

She told me that she reckoned I'd done such a good job looking after Melia that I deserved to be happy. I glowed all the rest of the day!

I went on glowing right through till Monday morning, when me and Melia set off for school and I started brooding all over again about Jem and Skye deserting me. Melia wanted to know if they were going to be there, and I had to say no. So then she wanted to know why not, and I said they just weren't, trying very hard not to snap cos after all it wasn't her fault. But oh, dear, she would persist!

"Why not, Frankie?" She tugged at my sleeve. "Why won't they be there?"

I said, "Because they won't."

"Why won't they?"

"Because—" I stopped.

"JEM!" shouted Melia. "SKYE!" They were waiting for us, on the corner. Melia went joyously galloping up. She threw her arms round Jem's neck.

"Frankie said you wouldn't be here!"

"Frankie was wrong," said Skye.

"Frankie was wrong!" Melia pointed an accusing finger at me. "She was wrong, she was wrong!"

We all walked down together to Melia's school. Melia hopped and skipped, and Skye never said a word. She didn't even purse her lips or make impatient tutting noises.

"See you later!" called Jem, as we dropped Melia off.

Melia gave one of her big banana beams and waved back. "See you later, albogator!"

"Albogator!" Jem giggled. "She's funny."

"Thought she embarrassed you," I said.

"Well, she does," agreed Skye, "but we talked about it, and we decided it wasn't fair, leaving you to cope on your own."

"Cos we are supposed to be your friends," said Jem.

"We *are* her friends."

"We are! We're your friends. And real true friends," said Jem, "are always there for each other."

"Always."

"Through thick and thin."

"We're just very sorry," said Skye, "that we weren't there on Saturday." She nudged at Jem. "Aren't we?"

Jem nodded. "We are! We're really, really sorry."

"Do you forgive us?" said Skye.

"*Please*, Frankie! Say you forgive us."

I mumbled that of course I did. "You don't have to *grovel*," I said.

"I do, I do!" Jem fell dramatically to her knees. "Look at me! Look at me grovelling!"

"I'd rather not," said Skye.

"Thing is..." Jem sprang back up again. "We didn't want you feeling that you had to start going round with someone like Daisy Hooper."

"God," I said, "I wouldn't go round with Daisy Hooper if she was the last person left on Earth! Not," I added, "that she is a person, strictly speaking. More like some kind of evil blob."

"Well, but you seemed to be getting all matey with Mel."

"Mel's all right," I said. "She doesn't hang with Daisy any more."

"First I heard of it," said Skye.

"No, she told me, she's gone right off her. She reckons she's mean."

"Tell us something we don't know!"

"Remember that girl at Juniors? Elsa Walker?"

"She ran away."

"Yes," I said, "and I know why."

"Why?" Jem danced in front of me. "Tell, tell!"

"According to Mel—"

"Wait!" Skye clapped her hands over her ears. "This is gossiping."

"Only about Daisy," said Jem. "If you don't want to hear, just walk on."

But of course Skye couldn't resist. She tries hard to be honourable and do what she knows is right, but Daisy has been our sworn enemy for as long as we can remember. It doesn't count as gossiping, I don't think. Not when you're talking about your sworn enemy.

"*Apparently,*" I said, "it was all down to Daisy, bullying her."

"She does that," said Jem. "She's always been a bully. She tried to bully me once."

"Really?"

"Way back in Reception. In the sandpit. She wanted my bucket and spade."

"Did you let her have them?"

"No, I bashed her!"

"Serve her right."

"Ought to be bashed more often," said Skye.

We wandered on happily through the school gates. I had the feeling we were back to normal.

On Saturday afternoon Mrs Duffy came to collect Melia, and by tea time I had moved back into my own little bedroom. I was so pleased to be there! It may be the size of a broom cupboard, but it is *mine*. And it is cosy. Being in Angel's room was like walking on egg shells, terrified all the time in case you broke something, or made marks on the carpet, or even just breathed a bit too heavily like poor old Melia had done.

In an odd sort of way, I found that I almost missed Melia. I suppose what it was, I had grown used to having her around. I missed her loud tuneless voice, and her big soppy beam. Rags missed her too. He kept trying to get into Angel's room to see if she was there. Even Skye missed her.

"It's strange, isn't it," she said, as we walked to school on our own on Monday morning, "not having Melia jumping about all over the place?"

"We ought to go down the road some time," suggested Jem, "and wave to her."

"I s'ppose we could," said Skye.

"Matter of fact," I said, "we've all been invited to tea next Saturday. Melia's mum wants to say thank you to us for looking after Melia."

There was a silence.

"You were the one that looked after her," said Skye. "We didn't do much."

"Didn't really do anything," said Jem.

"It'd seem like false pretences."

I guessed that meant they didn't want to come. I hadn't really thought they would. Having tea with Melia and her mum wasn't the most exciting prospect.

"Are you going to go?" said Jem.

"Couldn't very well get out of it," I said. "Didn't want to hurt Melia." And then I felt a bit ashamed. "Actually, I'm quite looking forward to it," I said. "I'm going to take Rags. He'll be so excited! He's really worried that he can't find her. He can't understand why she's not there any more. But it's all right," I said, "there's no need for you to come if you'd rather not. I can always tell Melia you're doing something else."

They looked at each other.

"Maybe we ought to come," said Skye.

"Yes, cos we are your friends," agreed Jem.

"Melia thinks you're her friends too." That's why she had asked them. She had no idea they found her an embarrassing nuisance.

"I suppose, in a way, she's right," said Skye.

"I know she used to get me really mad but you couldn't help feeling a bit fond of her."

"She could be really sweet," said Jem. "Like stealing that mug for your mum?"

"And d'you remember in Boots, that time, when she smeared lipstick all over herself?"

"And that time in HMV. I thought I'd die!"

"And then when she called Daisy *Snot Face*!"

"Omigod, yes!"

I didn't remind them that they hadn't found any of it very amusing when it was actually happening. I hadn't myself. But suddenly, we could all see the funny side.

"So does this mean you're going to come?" I said.

"Got to," said Jem. "Don't have any choice. Can't leave you on your own." She linked her arm through mine. "Told you before... real friends stick together!"

"Through thick and thin," said Skye.

We crammed three abreast through the main entrance, nearly knocking over Daisy Hooper as we did so. Things were *so* back to normal!

Back to normal at home, as well. I was in the kitchen with Mum, at tea time, when Angel came raging downstairs saying she had been checking up and *someone had messed with her things.* All because one of her china ornaments was facing the wrong way! Obviously the one poor old Melia had blown at.

"Someone's moved it!" shrieked Angel.

As a rule when Angel shrieks at me I shriek right back at her, but today, being in this exceptionally good mood, I simply, very calmly, said, "If that is so, then I apologise," which took the wind *right* out of her sails. She went all purple and started spluttering.

"Didn't I tell you, *don't touch anything?* Didn't I—"

"Oh, Angel, give it a rest," begged Mum.

"Leave your sister alone! She's had a lot to put up with these last few weeks. If you ask me –" she gave me a quick hug as she reached across for the kettle – "she deserves a medal! If all that's happened is one of your ornaments got turned the wrong way round, I don't reckon you have much to complain about."

Wow. It isn't very often Mum takes my side!

*Have you read the first
Frankie Foster?*

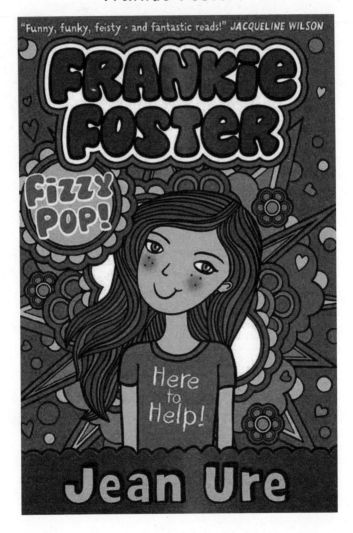

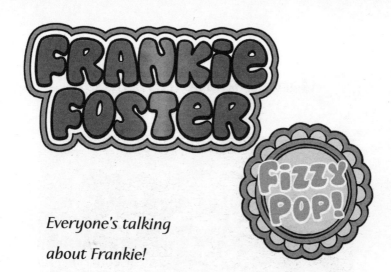

Everyone's talking
about Frankie!

"As soon as I opened *Fizzy Pop* I knew this was going to be a fantastic read! From the very first word Frankie spoke, I realised she was going to be my friend."
Imogen, age 12

"Original, funny and well-written, you just can't put *FizzyPop* down. I loved getting to know the characters through the story, especially Frankie, and her here-to-help attitude was really hilarious. The book was a real page-turner; I read it in one night it was that captivating."
Beth, age 9

"This book is addictive! It's funny and brilliant with great characters and a fantastic storyline. Frankie Foster's adventures are gripping with lots of twists – I could not put it down!"
Zoe, age 12

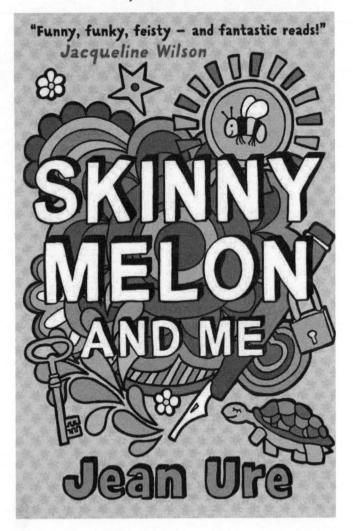

ICE LOLLY

Jean Ure

"Funny, funky, feisty – and fantastic reads!"
Jacqueline Wilson

FORTUNE COOKIE

Jean Ure

STAR CRAZY ME!

Jean Ure